GU00793049

To Maeve, fresh from Dub
old abbey', a heap of stones
in life, 'had nothing better t
backsides all day drawing letters made of snakes
eating their own tails.'

Her cousin, Leo, is very proud of it and its history.
Boy-next-door Jamie knows even more, and has an
ancient manuscript which starts them thinking ...

Then one dark night Leo makes his second sighting
of lights in the abbey grounds, and before Maeve
can say *'Faint Dioma'* she is dragged over the
fields to investigate.

They are certainly not prepared for what they see.

' "Do you think?" Leo swallowed hard. "Do you
think it might have been a ..."

'The same thought had occurred to me, but I didn't
want to dwell on it because I'd run screaming
from the place ...'

Mary Arrigan

dead monks
and
shady deals

Illustrated by Terry Myler

THE CHILDREN'S PRESS

To my son Conor,
with love

First published 1995 by
The Children's Press
45 Palmerston Road, Dublin 6.

© Text Mary Arrigan 1995
© Illustrations The Children's Press

ISBN 0 947962 91 3

Typeset by Computertype Limited
Printed by Colour Books Limited

Contents

1

Sent to the Country

The quietness, the smell of animals and old hay, the boredom; I could almost sense these things as I packed.

'I'll die,' I said to Mam, who was helping me. 'I'll simply curl up into a mindless ball and die. Why couldn't I go with you and Dad?'

'Because, for the umpteenth time,' she said, 'your uncle Josh only sent tickets for your dad and me to fly over. You, my whining little bear cub, are not invited. It's an adult wedding.'

Josh is my dad's younger brother. He went to America at nineteen and made pots of money as a tailor. Now he was getting married. You'd think, with all that wealth, he'd have invited me too. But no; the stingy creep. No more Christmas cards from this niece, that's for sure.

'Pack your anorak and wellies,' Mam was saying.

'I won't be going out much,' I sighed. 'I expect I'll just sit in and watch telly mostly. Agricultural air makes me ill.'

Mam threw a sweater at me. 'Cheeky brat,' she laughed. That's the thing about Mam, she rarely gets rattled. I'd have to try harder.

'You're abandoning your only child while you go swanning off across the world. You'll feel guilty and miserable before the plane even takes off.'

She laughed again. 'Guilty? You must be joking, Maeve Morris.' And she pushed me on to my bed and tickled me until I screamed. Very undignified for a grown woman, not to mention her thirteen-year-old daughter.

So, here I was on the train, speeding away from civilisation. What, I asked myself, am I going to do for fun over the next two weeks in my Aunt Brid's? I pondered on this as I sipped the very expensive and yukky coffee I'd bought from a fellow pushing a trolley along the train.

My Aunt Brid is a pretty decent sort. She's Mam's sister and she runs a market garden. Jim is her second husband and he runs a small restaurant in the town of Kildioma, two miles away. He calls it Jim's Kitchen. What a name – no class. They have a baby called Miriam who pukes and pees and wears her dinner on her head. Then there's my cousin, Leo. He's Aunt Brid's son by her first marriage. He's almost eleven, a mere child. No point in depending on his company, I thought. He'll be building bird-houses and reading books. He's always looking after twittering birds or else nursing some half-dead creature he's picked up from the road. Either that or he's poring over a mega-boring tome with hundreds of *useful facts* scattered about in it. I mean I could understand if he read books with swashbuckling heroes dashing about lopping the heads off criminals and dragons and stuff, but imagine anyone enjoying books about *facts!*

'I'll be brain dead by the end of this July,' I almost said out loud, wondering where I'd dispose of the paper cup half full of the train fuel they used for coffee. I could see my reflection on the window as the train clattered through a tunnel. I looked like a romantic heroine, pining and dejected, speeding to a fate of utter misery.

The beautiful young Miss Morris sighed. Her mother had

died of consumption and her father had died of plague while in prison for gambling debts. The Country Mansion had been sold, to pay those same debts, to an upstart tradesman who'd made his fortune from hair-oil. As she listened to the rhythmic clatter of the horses' hooves as the coach swept her to her destiny, Miss Morris delicately wiped a tear with the corner of her lace hanky. What would it be like, this Darkling Hall, where she was to take up the post of governess to a young, orphaned boy with a withered foot?

The coach drew to a halt and the horses snorted with impatience. But hark, who was this approaching? Why it was none other than Lord Chiselchin, the boy's guardian. She could almost hear his manly heart thumping beneath his brocade waistcoat. He spoke ...

'Ticket please, miss.'

2

The Boy with the Fair Isle Jumper

'You must be starving,' Aunt Brid said when I came down to the kitchen after unpacking. Leo was washing his hands at the sink, and Miriam was in her high chair trying to knock over one of those non-spill cups.

'I am,' I said. 'Ravenous.'

Jim plonked a casserole dish on the table and took the lid off. A cloud of delicious smelling steam made my mouth water. Staying with a chef just might compensate for the disadvantages of being exiled into isolation.

'I hope you like vegetarian food,' said Aunt Brid, ladling out a brown concoction on to my plate'

'What?' Perhaps I'd picked it up wrong; I sometimes have difficulty with words of more than one syllable.

'We've gone vegetarian,' she announced. 'It's much healthier.'

'You have?' I choked. Great, on top of everything else I was landed with a bunch of health-food freaks. Leo was grinning. He was enjoying my discomfort, the little wimp.

Jim smiled. 'It's really nice when you get used to it.'

'I doubt if I'll live that long,' I muttered, poking at the mess on my plate. Aunt Brid laughed. Like her sister, she rarely gets rattled. 'Here, try it with a piece of garlic bread.'

The beautiful Miss Morris sat alone in her attic bedroom and looked at the tray that jealous Miss Pickaxe, the housekeeper, had brought. Stale bread and sour milk again.

Now that his lordship had left to do business in the city, the housekeeper, jealous of the young governess's beauty and superior brain, chose to stint on the victuals and basic creature comforts.

'Oh woe is me,' sobbed the hapless maiden. 'Poor wretch that I am – abandoned, poor and hungry.'

'I know you'll like the pudding,' Jim was saying. 'Fresh strawberry mousse.'

It was great, but I didn't show my enthusiasm; it would have undone all my misery.

'Would you like to come to town with me, the two of you?' Jim asked. 'I can drop you off at the square and pick you up later.'

I was about to agree to this offer. Kildioma is a snoring-boring little midlands town that boasts a grotty old ruined castle and a museum, but at least there was a fine shopping centre where one could hang out and spot biker dudes – if such things had reached this godforsaken pit. Before I could say a word, Leo snapped an answer.

'We're going to the abbey'

My jaw fell slack with shock. Did he really think I'd pass up a lift to civilisation, however primitive, to go to his stupid old abbey?

'Hold on a sec,' I began.

Leo stood up, his eyes never leaving Jim. 'We're going to the abbey,' he said again. Something in his manner sent warning bells a-jangle in my head, so I shut my mouth. Jim simply shrugged and glanced at Aunt Brid. She frowned and sighed, but neither of them said anything. There was obviously something heavy going on here, so 'Proceed with caution, Maeve,' flashed into the floppy disk in my brain.

'You're nuts, you know,' I said to Leo when we were outside together. 'Passing up a couple of hours in beautiful downtown Kildioma, gateway to the cosmos, just to go to the cruddy old abbey.'

'I thought you liked it,' Leo growled. He's very proud of the old ruined abbey across the field from the house.

'Not really,' I said. 'I've seen it hundreds of times. It's just a heap of stones and dead monks. We might have had a bit of fun in town. Why wouldn't you take up Jim's offer, you twit?'

'Wouldn't give him the satisfaction,' muttered Leo.

'What do you mean?'

'Never mind. None of your business,' and he ran ahead of me across the field.

Stupid abbey, I thought, puffing to catch up with him. Who cares if monks lived there hundreds of years ago, writing books that nobody can read and hacking crosses out of chunks of stone. Daft bunch of men with funny hairstyles and ridiculous rules about women.

Leo grinned and waited for me, the sunlight glinting on one of those oversized watches that tells you what time it is in Katmandu.

'I bet you're scared. I bet you think the ghosts of the monks will rise up and drag you into their clutches. Maeve is a scaredy-cat!'

'You watch too many horror movies, little boy,' I scoffed. 'Anyway, if there was something to be scared about at least it would make the place interesting.'

There was a man at the abbey when we arrived. We didn't mind; lots of tourists with nothing better to do often come to mooch around. Except that this man wasn't looking at the carvings on the doorway nor the high cross. He just had his hands in this pockets and was kicking the gravel with scruffy trainers. He was wearing a lumberjack shirt that I'd have liked for myself. You could say that he sported designer stubble, like those sexy tennis players, but personally I'd say that he just hadn't bothered to shave.

'Hello,' said Leo. He's like that. I suppose living in the country does that to you – makes you so glad to see anyone that you'll gabble to them. We don't do that in the city.

The man nodded and muttered something.

'He's really pleased to see us,' I whispered to Leo.

'Maybe he's a film producer,' said Leo. 'Looking around for a location for his film – NIGHTMARE AT THE OLD ABBEY.'

'MONKBUSTERS,' I giggled.

'ATTACK OF THE KILLER MONKS!' Leo was losing the run of himself.

'JURASSIC PARK MEETS THE MONKS!' I always like to get the last word.

'That doesn't make sense ...' began Leo.

'Oh, come on,' I said. 'Let's sneak into McLaren's place.'

Mr McLaren trains racehorses and owns the estate on the far side of the abbey. He also owns the land that the abbey is on, but there's some sort of arrangement with the government people who do monuments and that stuff which allows access to the place. You can actually see the house through the trees from Aunt Brid's bathroom window. Years before, Leo and I had discovered a hole in the high stone wall surrounding the estate, and we often crept through to spy.

'I hope we get chased,' said Leo as we made our way through the laurel bushes.

'Not me,' I said. 'Can't you imagine the scene in the school yard: "And what was the highlight of your holiday, Maeve?" "Oh, getting chased by a very old gardener while trespassing." My friends would be really under-awed by that.'

The laurel bushes stopped at a smooth lawn which led to the back of the house. The French window was open and we could hear a piano playing.

'That's Chopsticks,' said Leo. 'My ma can play that.'

'What a cultured lad you are,' I said, 'to be able to recognise classical tunes like Chopsticks.'

'Drop dead,' said Leo.

The music stopped and a boy came out on to the

patio, followed by one of those honey-coloured dogs that fetch dead things which people shoot for sport.

'Who's he?' I'd never seen him before.

'He must be old McLaren's grandson. I heard he had one, but I've never seen him.'

The boy was wearing a Fair Isle jumper like you see in women's magazines: 'Knit this Fabulous Puce Sweater for the Man in Your Life' or 'Knit your own Royal Family in Pure New Wool.'

'Looks a bit of a nancy,' I said.

'Oh, belt up,' said Leo. 'Always ready to knock people, aren't you? You never give anyone a chance. You make me sick.'

'Well, just look at his jumper ...' I began.

'Phooey. Just because someone is not dressed in heavy metal gear doesn't make him a nancy.'

The dog stopped and looked in our direction. Before we could move, he was crashing through the laurel bushes to where we were crouching. Now, I'm not exactly afraid of dogs, but I like to keep my distance, you understand. So, when this heap of canine flesh thundered at us, I screamed.

'Stupid twit,' growled Leo.

'Who's there?' the boy called out. Very posh accent, wouldn't you know. Very plummy indeed. 'Come here, Groucho.' But Groucho was pleased with the new company and was jumping around us. I grabbed Leo and held him between me and the dog. Desperation makes you ruthless; better a maimed cousin than a maimed me. The boy peered at us through the bushes.

'Who are you? Don't you know this is private property?'

'My good man,' I said, restoring myself to the dignity of an upright position. 'We've been for a walk and seem to have taken a wrong turn.'

'Through a thick laurel hedge?' the boy laughed. He had nice teeth and his eyes crinkled up when he laughed. Pity about the accent. 'Pull the other leg.'

'We were just having a look,' said Leo, honest as usual. 'We didn't mean any harm.'

'Yes we did.' I don't like being laughed at. 'We were casing the joint. We intended coming back tonight to steal your ... your knitwear. For a scarecrow we're making.'

The boy blushed and looked down at his Fair Isle jumper. 'Very funny,' he said. 'Very droll and witty. And what institution let you out for the day?'

Leo hooted with laughter. 'Oh, I love that,' he chortled unkindly. 'I must remember that. That'll teach you, Maeve.'

'I'm Jamie Stephenson,' said the boy, more pally now that he had Leo's approval. 'Who are you two?'

'I'm Leo. And she's not my sister, she's just a cousin. Her name is Maeve.'

'From the city of Dublin,' I added, to establish my superior status.

Jamie sat on a curvy branch to talk to us. Like I said, country people are like that; confront them with another human being and life stories will be exchanged before you know it. It comes of being surrounded by fields and country stuff. Anyway, this Jamie told us his father was in the army, out with the United Nations keeping the peace in one of those unpronounceable countries.

'He's on leave at the moment, in Paris. Mum's gone to

have a holiday with him. That's why I'm here with my grandad.'

'A rejected offspring, just like me,' I sighed. 'Unloved and unwanted while they whoop it up.'

'Ignore her,' said Leo with what I thought was a hurtful lack of loyalty.

'And grandad doesn't even have a video,' added Jamie.

'Wow!' I empathised. 'My lot don't even have MTV. Mega-boredom.' Here was a kindred spirit – probably even worse off than I. At least I had Leo to torment and keep my mind off my misery.

'Big deal,' scoffed Leo. But I knew he'd been campaigning for satellite for ages, so his remark didn't ring true.

'Why don't you hang about with us?' I invited Jamie. Call me impulsive, but he seemed so lonely that the words just spilled out.

'Yeah,' enthused Leo. 'I could sure do with some decent company.'

I ignored that and looked expectantly at Jamie. He wasn't leaping about at my suggestion. In fact his face had clouded and he was shuffling his feet. 'I'm afraid my grandad is a bit protective. I get to go to Limerick or Dublin with him a couple of times a week, but other than that I have to stay within our grounds.'

'That's a bore,' said Leo. 'He must think you're made of china or something, that you'll break easily.'

'Oh, it's just that he reads about IRA kidnappings and things,' sighed Jamie.

'There's no IRA around here,' said Leo. 'Besides, that's all over now. All that trouble in the North is finished since they declared peace.'

'Anyway why would they want to kidnap you?' I asked.

'Because Mr. McLaren is maggoty rich, isn't that right, Jamie?' said Leo.

Jamie shrugged. 'Used to be,' he said. 'But now, with the upkeep of the big old house and the horses and grounds, he's feeling the pinch a bit. People seem to think he's better off than he really is. Still, it doesn't stop him being over-protective towards me. It's silly really. Nobody around here even knows me. Grandad is such a fusspot.'

'Listen, I have an idea,' said Leo. 'Why don't we meet you here every day? We'll find something to do, the three of us.'

Jamie's face lit up. 'That would be great!'

Not to be outdone, I put in my spoke. 'We could do a bit of exploring. Maybe even take in a swim in the lake behind the woods. You'd be back before they knew you'd gone.'

'Great,' he laughed. 'Right on. Let's do that.'

'How old are you?' asked Leo, making sure the candidate qualified for our company.

'Thirteen and a half.'

'That's all right then,' said Leo.

'Why don't we go now?' I said. 'No point in wasting time.'

'Yes. We could go to the abbey,' said Leo.

'Oh no. Not the crummy abbey again,' I groaned.

'OK,' Jamie glanced back at the house. 'Grandad's down at the stables. Let's go then. Come on, Groucho.'

3

Lights at the Abbey

'Have you seen this place before?' I asked Jamie as we neared the abbey.

'No. My dad gets moved around quite a bit, so we haven't been in Ireland since I was small.'

'Monks built it,' said Leo, pointing to the ruin. 'We did a project about it in school. A fellow called Saint Dioma lived in a wooden hut here over a thousand years ago. This stone abbey was founded later in the twelfth century on the same site.'

'How amazingly mind-boggling,' I said. 'And this is Saint Maeve of the late twentieth century bored mindless on the same site. Come on, let's go down to the woods.'

'No, I'd like to see the ruins,' said Jamie. I could see Leo gloating. He always does that when he gets his way.

'Well, you two go in and look at the mouldy old place. I'll stay here in the sunshine.' I wasn't about to give in. I sat on the grass outside the abbey with Groucho while the other two blew their minds with the aura of the long dead.

'You and me, Groucho, we're the only sane ones in this lot.' I reached out and patted his head. He was scrabbling at something in the grass. 'What have you got there, boy?'

He looked up at me and dropped what he had in his mouth. It was a brass button with the insignia of a yacht on it. Just the sort of thing a twelfth-century monk would use to hold up his drawers. I put it in my pocket. I hoard things that I find – you'd never know when they might come in handy. I have a box at home where I keep things like that. Ma says I'll come back in my next life as a squirrel with buck teeth, red hair and given to storing nuts in trees. Charming old lady, my mother. I looked up as the other two came out through the arched doorway.

'Jamie says there's a book about this place in his grandad's library,' Leo said.

Jamie nodded. 'I've seen it in the glass case where grandad keeps the old, rare books. It's a manuscript actually; written by hand. It's called *A History of Saint Dioma's Abbey.*'

'Well, Mr Encyclopaedia, will you give us a look at this book?' I asked.

Jamie was embarrassed. 'I'm not allowed to touch the ones in the glass case,' he said. Then, before I could call him nancy, he added, 'Oh hell, all right. I'll sneak you into the library tomorrow. Grandad hardly ever goes in there. Anyway he's going to some race-meeting in the afternoon. I'll tell him I don't want to go.'

Good, I thought. A chance to see inside the manor house that Leo and I had made up so many stories about when we were younger. Stories about demented ancestors who roamed the dreary corridors at night, wailing spirits that caused the face of anyone who saw them to twist into permanent deformation. I used to enjoy frightening the bejapers out of Leo by turning my eyelids inside out and screaming that I'd seen a lost soul outside.

Jamie was looking at his watch. 'Look at the time,' he said. 'The afternoon flew. I'd better go. Dinner's at six.'

'What are you having?' I asked.

'I think it's chicken.'

'God,' I sighed. 'I'd kill for chicken leg with nice, crispy skin. What are we having for tea, Leo?' I turned to my cousin. 'Braised lettuce? Stuffed pea? Roast cabbage?'

'Leave off, Maeve.' Leo was angry and embarrassed. Oops, I'd gone too far. He wasn't responsible for his freaky folks. 'Sorry,' I said. 'I'm just not used to veggie stuff.' The moment passed.

'I'll be off,' said Jamie. 'See you tomorrow.'

'What time will we come?' asked Leo.

'I think it would be safe to come around two. Grandad will be well gone by then. I'll meet you in the laurels at two then, OK?'

'It sounds like a conspiracy,' I laughed.

'A what?' asked Leo.

'Never mind.' It would have taken too much energy to explain. There was a BMW parked in the yard when we got home. Aunt Brid was talking to a short, bald man with a moon face and pink eyelids. He was wearing one of those navy blazers that old wrinklies think of as trendy; the sort my mother would call 'well turned out'. His pale-coloured trousers had creases that would cut through steel, but in spite of that he looked like an old droopy drawers.

'Well, just think about it,' the man was saying as he got into his car.

'That's Mr O'Rourke,' Leo said to me. 'He's an auctioneer in town. He owns the land beyond our house, keeps cattle on it. What did he want, Mam?'

Aunt Brid laughed. 'Funny thing,' she said. 'He arrived here out of the blue to ask if we'd consider selling out. Cheek!'

'And will you sell?' I asked hopefully. Perhaps she'd see the light and move closer to civilisation. Anyway you'd want to be a fool not to see that they were barely existing on the money they got from the market garden and the restaurant. Especially a *vegetarian* restaurant, for goodness sake.

'Not likely,' said Aunt Brid. 'Not bloomin' likely. Jim and I have done up this cottage and garden exactly as we dreamed. We wouldn't part with it for anything. It ... it's our bit of heaven.'

Heaven! Two miles from town with nothing between here and human contact but a grotty ruin and the stuffy McLaren place (which couldn't be seen from the road anyway). The road on the other side of the cottage simply led to O'Rourke's fields, the forest and the bog. A dead end in every sense. If this was heaven, I'd happily settle for the other place.

'I'll tell Jim when he comes home,' said Aunt Brid. 'It will give him a laugh.'

'Yeah, do that,' Leo muttered under his breath. 'Let's make Jim laugh.'

If Aunt Brid heard, she didn't pretend. But you could sense a sudden coldness in the atmosphere.

'Creep,' I hissed at Leo.

'Mind your own stupid business.' His eyes glittered dangerously as he turned to me. This was a side of Leo I had never seen before. I pulled a face just to let him see who was superior, but I kept my mouth shut.

Later that evening Jim handed the newspaper he was reading to Aunt Brid.

'Look at that,' he said. 'Another ancient slab missing.'

Brid looked at the article and tut-tutted. 'An eighth-century incised slab,' she read. 'From Clonfraoch Abbey. That's only seven miles from here. Shame.'

'Who'd want to take a hunk of battered old stone?' I asked, helping myself to another dollop of apple meringue that Jim had brought from the restaurant.

'You'd be surprised,' said Jim. 'Buying and selling items of rare, historic interest has become big business.'

'That's daft!' I could think of better things to do with money.

'Well, someone's making a packet of money out of these thefts,' put in Aunt Brid. 'The sort of people with no pride in our heritage. They'd sell their grannies for a fast buck.'

'Speaking of fast bucks, or even slow ones, I'd better go. I've an evening menu to prepare,' Jim said, getting up from the table. 'This is my late-opening night.'

Jim's Kitchen wasn't one of those fancy night spots. It was really a snackery which specialised in things like homemade soup, pasta stuff, salad things, brown bread and pretty decent desserts. His busiest time was during the lunch period when the people who worked in the offices and shops in town wanted a light meal. Thursday night was late opening in the shopping centre and Jim stayed open to catch the late shoppers.

'Could I come, Jim?' I asked eagerly. 'I'd be a super waitress.' Here was a chance to get away for the night. And meet people. And get fat tips.

Jim laughed and patted my head. 'I'm sure you would, sunshine. But there's a law against employing thirteen-year-olds.'

I hate being treated like a child. It makes me want to shock. 'I could go topless. That would pull the crowds.'

'Topless!' Leo shrieked. 'I'd look better topless than you. You're built like a drainpipe.'

'Well at least I'm a tall drainpipe,' I snorted. Leo hates jokes about his lack of height, which makes it very easy to insult him when he asks for it. Anyway, if I hunch my shoulders I can look really busty.

'Cheerio, folks,' said Jim, taking his coat off the back of his chair. I kind of felt sorry for him. All that hard work and long hours.

'Bye,' said myself and Aunt Brid. Leo just gazed out of the window. Jim looked at him expectantly for a moment, then went out. Aunt Brid looked like she was about to say something, but she just pursed her lips and set about wiping Miriam's hands. Rude little prat, that Leo, I thought, scowling across at him.

That night I went into Leo's room to get an Asterix book from his collection.

'Look,' I said, glancing out of the window. 'There are lights around the abbey.'

Leo peered out. 'It's probably fellows lamping foxes,' he said.

'Whatting foxes?'

'Lamping foxes. They shine a powerful light into the

fox's eyes to dazzle him. Then they shoot him and get money for the skin.'

'That's horrible. I've never heard anything so disgusting. I'd like to go down there and give them a piece of my mind.'

Leo laughed. 'You've none to spare. Besides, it would make no difference to the likes of them. Though I don't think they'll catch anything, those lights are too dim.'

'Leo, Maeve! Are you two still yapping? It's eleven thirty,' Aunt Brid called from downstairs. Although the house was a cottage, Jim had made two really groovy bedrooms out of the attic. The ceilings were slanted and the windows were set into little niches with cushioned seats.

'Bed! Now!' insisted Aunt Brid. I scarpered across the narrow landing to my room and dived under the duvet.

The beautiful Miss Morris blew out the candle and tucked the threadbare blanket around her delicate shoulders. She dreamed of young Lord Chiselchin. Her heart fluttered and she brushed away a tear as she dwelled on the loneliness of one so handsome, so troubled by cruel fate. What awful shadow prevented him from seeing the brightness of life? Across the dark hall, the little boy with the withered foot stirred in his sleep and called out a heart-rending wail of anguish.

'Leo! Turn down that bloody music,' shouted Aunt Brid. 'Use your walkman if you must listen to that rave rubbish at this hour of the night.'

4

Gorgeous Fergus

The next afternoon we met Jamie as planned, in the laurel bushes. He was waiting for us and he grinned when he saw us coming.

'Glad you could make it,' he said.

'Of course we could make it,' I laughed. 'It's not as if there were any scintillatingly exciting events to prevent us from coming here. Are you going to let us into your grandad's library?'

Jamie nodded. 'Come on,' he said. 'Just don't make noise in case Mrs O'Toole, the housekeeper, goes on the prowl.'

'Why have you got a housekeeper?' asked Leo, pushing through the bushes after Jamie. 'Have you no granny?'

Jamie held a branch to let me pass. 'My granny lives in London,' he said. 'She left here ... left grandad years ago. I usually stay with her whenever my folks are away, but she's gone on holidays with a Norwegian fisherman.'

'Groovy,' I said. 'Actually,' I added as we crossed the smooth lawn and I'd had time to think, 'our granny lives with a Galway motor magnate.'

Leo looked at me, his eyes and mouth wide open. I tried to signal to him to leave my interesting statement alone, but could he? No, not Leo.

'You're out of your tiny mind,' he laughed. 'Our granny is married to our grandad and they own a small shop with a petrol pump. Grandad would throw a fit if he heard you call him a motor magnate. You snobby clown.'

'Oh, well, anyway,' I muttered. I hoped my face wasn't as red on the outside as it felt on the inside.

The double glass doors leading into the library were open. Jamie turned to us before going in.

'Don't ... er ... don't touch anything,' he said.

I froze and put my hands on my hips.

'Just what do you think we are? Some sort of grunting half-wits who don't know books from ... from loo paper? If you think we're just coming in to thrash your ould grandad's mouldy books, well think again.'

Leo looked perplexed. He could see that I was defending his honour as well as my own, but still he wanted to see the book about the abbey.

'Sorry,' said Jamie. 'I didn't mean ... it's just that grandad is very organised and he'd know if anyone was messing about with his books. He'd bawl me out if he knew ... I'm really sorry.'

'Yeah, well,' I muttered.

Leo looked relieved and we stepped across the threshold into the library. It was cool and dark. There was a smell of tobacco and old leather. The wooden floor was so shiny you could see the reflection of the furniture as if there was another upside-down room underneath. The four walls were covered with shelves of books and there was a spiral stairs which led to an upper gallery where there were more bookshelves.

'Wow!' whispered Leo. 'You'd want to be locked in here for about ninety years to get through all those words.'

'"Want" is hardly the word I'd use, sunshine,' I said. 'Maybe a wimp like you would *want* to smother in those old tomes, but normal people like me were created for better things.'

Leo ignored me. 'Does he read all these, your grandad?' he continued.

Jamie shrugged. 'Some. He likes reading and he knows a lot about everything. But I think most of them are just an investment. There's money in rare books.'

He reached up and took down a thin leather-covered book from a glass case. It wasn't bound like ordinary books; it was held together by big stitches. 'This is it. This is the one I told you about, the history of the abbey.'

He set it down on the floor and we crouched beside him as he turned the pages. It was the sort of book you see when the credits are rolling in those old-fashioned horror movies, all gothic writing and frayed edges. The print was brownish and there were sketches and plans of the abbey. Not the sort of book you'd take to bed with your cornflakes and cocoa. In fact, a boring looking tome, but I wasn't about to say so. One has one's pride.

'See, here's the story of the founding of the abbey,' Jamie was saying. "It was originally a wooden construction in the seventh century. St Dioma lived here for a while before he went to settle in Antrim. He started the Book of Dimma which is in Trinity College now. That's what monks did in those days. They made books called illuminated manuscripts ...'

'Like the Book of Kells,' interrupted Leo. 'That's in Trinity College too.'

'Right,' said Jamie, turning the page. 'Look, Dimma is another name for Dioma. That's why the book is called the Book of Dimma.'

'Had they nothing better to do than sit on their backsides all day drawing letters made of snakes eating their own tails?' I snorted. 'Anyway we came to find out about the abbey, not some antediluvian monk with a name like a light-bulb.'

Leo laughed with a superior-sounding shriek. 'He couldn't be an antediluvian monk,' he jeered. 'Antediluvian means "before the Flood" and the Flood was way before Christianity. How could you have a monk before ...?'

'Ah, shut up, knowall,' I snapped. 'I was just testing to see if you knew ...'

'Can we get back to the book?' Jamie peered up at the two of us. Leo put his head down again to look at it.

'Faint Dioma?' he pointed to the words. 'Why was he faint?'

'Saint,' Jamie laughed. 'It's Saint Dioma. That's the way they used to write the letter S in the seventeen hundreds.'

'The filly fods,' I said.

'Look,' Leo added. 'High croff.'

'Fouth-facing wall,' Jamie joined in.

'Earlier fite.'

'Fecret chamber.'

'What?' Jamie and I said together.

'Fecret chamber,' repeated Leo, pointing his grimy finger at the page. 'See, that's what it says.'

Sure enough, on a plan of the abbey there was an arrow pointing to a secret chamber under the chancel – that's the part of the church where the altar is.

'I wonder if it's still there,' I said.

'Wouldn't that be brilliant!' exclaimed Leo. 'We might find a hoard of chalices and stuff and get millions. Like those people in Derrynaflan who found things like that

years ago. They got loads of money as a reward.'

'Let's go right now and see.' I must admit I was caught up in his enthusiasm.

'Hello. What have we here?' A shadow fell across the doorway and the three of us jumped.

'Oh cripes!' I gasped. 'Your grandad. Now the sh ... now the muck's hit the fan.'

Jamie's flustered expression changed to one of relief. 'It's OK,' he said, closing the book. 'It's only Fergus.'

Fergus stepped out of the light and came towards us. Now that I could see him clearly, my heart did a double somersault; he was only drop-dead gorgeous. It was as if every mega-star of the rock world had been compressed into one fantastic body. He wore a black tee-shirt which showed off every sculpted muscle on his torso. His tight jeans showed no evidence of either a beer-belly or baggy-bum. But it was his face that made my knees turn to jelly. He was like a granite-faced angel – perfect enough to be angelic yet rough enough to be heroically masculine. The slight scar under his cheek gave him an air of mystery. If I was God I'd make all men like this.

The beautiful Miss Morris looked up from her classy book as young Lord Chiselchin entered the conservatory.

'Miss Morris,' he said, plucking a rose from a nearby bush. 'I trust you like it here at Darkling Hall. I must apologise for my long absences, but business denies me the pleasure of the company of my ward and ... and your charming self. Young Edward has blossomed since your arrival. You have worked wonders with him.'

Miss Morris laid down the book and smiled gratefully at her employer.

'I love the dear boy, Lord Chiselchin,' she murmured. 'And I love this place.' She didn't add that the rest of the staff made her life a misery while the Master was away. Nothing must upset this moment. She reached out to accept the proffered rose and, briefly, her fingers touched his. 'Thank you,' she whispered as she gazed into his grey eyes. She noticed the scar under his cheek. He'd probably got that fighting a duel in the interest of justice.

'Get off me foot, you nelly.'

'What?'

'Me foot,' repeated Leo. 'You're sitting on me foot.

And your mouth is hanging open like a gargoyle's.'

I scrambled to my feet, my gaze never leaving Lord ... never leaving Fergus's face.

'This is Leo and his cousin Maeve,' Jamie was saying. 'We're just looking at one of grandad's old books.'

'You'll catch it if he ever finds out,' Fergus grinned, showing off white, even teeth.

'Well, you're not going to tell him, are you?' muttered Jamie, replacing the book. 'Anyway, you shouldn't be here either ... Fergus is new here,' he explained, turning towards Leo and me, 'he looks after the horses.'

I tried to smile gently and murmur a sexy 'How nice.' But all I could manage was a strangled 'Miff' and a sickly idiotic grin. I hoped it was too dark for him to notice.

'Which book were you looking at?' Fergus asked.

'One about the abbey,' put in Jamie in an off-hand way.

'It's got a secret chamber and there could be treasure ...' began Leo.

'Shut up,' I hissed, nudging him in the back. I didn't want Fergus thinking we were some sort of looney kids.

'Secret chamber? In the old abbey?' Fergus threw back his head and laughed. 'That would be a fine thing. You'd be wasting your time looking for anything in that place. All you'd find is a few rotten bones and a summons from the Office of Public Works for interfering with an ancient monument. Treasure, my eye. Anything like that would have been found centuries ago – if it was there in the first place. And it wasn't. It's just a heap of stones.'

My sentiments entirely. Not alone was this man a perfect specimen of hunkdom, but he had a superior mind like my own. Being stuck in the country might begin to pay dividends after all.

'Leave those mouldy books alone and get out into the fresh air,' said Fergus. 'Would any of you folks like to ride Daisy?'

'Daisy?' scoffed Jamie. 'She's a million years old and creaks when she moves.'

'She moves well and, besides, it's good for her to be ridden. She's a good horse for beginners.'

I bristled slightly. How did he know Leo and I were beginners? For all he knew we could have been champions of the Dublin Horse Show or Dressage – that stupid thing where they make horses dance sideways to frilly music. But I let it pass. Anyway, if he was offering us a ride, it would mean spending time in his company and that was fine by me.

'We'd love to ride Daisy,' I said. 'Sounds better than being stuck indoors.'

Fergus grinned at me and fireworks coursed through every artery in my body as we followed him outside.

The stable yard was square and cobbled with stalls around three sides. Horses looked out at us over some of the half doors on which their names were written – Beauty of the Glen, Ice Cream, Adelaide Rose and other weird titles. An old groom was mucking out one of the stables. He was small and skinny and had a bony, bald head. He looked up and frowned at us.

'Just giving the younsters a ride,' Fergus shouted to him. The old geezer's face tightened like a distressed prune. He ignored us.

'What's eating Prince Charming there?' I asked Jamie. Jamie grinned.

'That's Reilly,' he said. 'He's been grandad's right-hand man since the year dot and thinks Fergus is an upstart.'

'Jealous old fogey,' I muttered.

Fergus opened one of the doors and led out an impossibly high creature.

'I thought you said she was old if not decrepit,' I whispered to Jamie.

'She is,' he said.

She looked awfully lively to me. I nudged Leo. 'Now, Leo,' I said graciously. 'You've always wanted to ride a horse. Here's your chance.'

But Fergus held out his hand to me. 'Ladies first, I think.'

'Hell,' I thought as I looked way up into the eyes of Daisy, 'this monster is going to kill me, but I'll die in the arms of Fab Fergus. Good-bye, world.'

Let me just gloss hastily over the first few disastrous attempts at staying aboard this hippo on mile-high stilts. It would do nothing for the story nor my dignity to dwell on matters of fear and cowardice. I'll just proceed to the bragging stage where I can say that, by the end of the afternoon, with Fergus's confident coaching and my own steely will-power, I could manage to trot around the yard with a fair degree of non-panic.

Later, as we made for home across the fields, I even felt benign towards Leo. Fergus had said that he'd give us another riding-lesson tomorrow afternoon. I had found True Love and I could ride a horse. God was beginning to squint in my direction.

5

Mr O'Rourke Makes an Offer

'How about a bit of weeding, you two?' Aunt Brid asked after breakfast next morning. I was saved from answering because I was chewing her home-made muesli which takes forever to get to the swallowing stage. The spit-making parts of my mouth had never had so much exercise.

'Oh,' said Leo. 'I thought Maeve and I could walk into town.'

Walk! Did he say walk? Put one foot in front of the other with regular monotony for two whole miles? Not me, kid.

Jim smiled as he rose from the table. 'Got to earn your keep, you two,' he said.

I practically choked. Here I was, surviving on sawdust and bird turds, and he called it 'keep'!

'I'd really appreciate it,' put in Aunt Brid. Leo looked at me and I shrugged to make it look like I agreed. I didn't want to go to town anyway. I wanted to save my energy and fresh good looks for Fergus in the afternoon.

'I'll help with the weeding if you'll lend me your walkman,' I said to Leo later as we cleared the table. 'Otherwise you're on your own. I'm a visitor and I don't have to do chores like that.'

'You'll waste my batteries,' he began.

'It was my idea to go to the McLaren place and we met Jamie and Fergus, remember? Only for me we wouldn't have new friends and riding-lessons. If you go on to be a champion jockey, you'll have me to thank.'

'Oh well, all right. Though that's blackmail.'

I smiled charmingly as I popped in my new Pearl Jam tape.

There's nothing so boring as weeding. I'd have preferred to dig up the sprouts and other stuff and leave the weeds, but I'm much too good-natured to upset Aunt Brid – especially when she needed any money she got for the veggies which she sold to local shops, as well as supplying Jim's restaurant. However the agony wasn't so bad when I had the walkman going. Music soothes the savage whatsit and all that.

The beautiful Miss Morris could feel the wind rushing through her lustrous, long hair as she galloped over the moor on Dais ... on Monarch, the fastest horse in the stable.

She had lain, tossing and turning in her bed in the hours before daylight. Then she sought to cool her fevered mind by taking Monarch for a run. She felt so helpless, seeing the troubled features of her beloved Lord Chiselchin on his infrequent visits to his estate. When he did come home, he seemed to spend most of his time in his study. What business took him to the city and made him so miserable when he came back? If only she could help.

'Hup, Monarch,' she said. Perhaps this ride would calm her anxiety. A gifted horsewoman, she kept the lively stallion firmly under control. Her heart fluttered as the cold dawn wind chilled her beautiful features. Her ride took her to the cliffs, away at the north end of the estate. She stopped to watch the dawn appear over the horizon and was surprised when she heard voices below. Creeping to the edge of the cliff, she gasped when she saw a group of people below in the cove,

carrying heavy crates from a boat and disappearing into what must be a cave, out of her line of vision.

Smugglers! she thought. There was a lot of it about, according to the newspapers. She gasped again as she recognised Pickaxe and her scumbag nephew; Snarl, the under-gardener; and some others from Lord Chiselchin's household. The rotten lot – using their employer's estate to conceal their criminal activities. She must get back to Darkling Hall to warn his lordship. As she turned, her foot dislodged a stone which went crashing down the cliff with a loud clatter.

The group below looked up. A grimace of recognition crossed Pickaxe's evil face. Miss Morris quickly mounted Monarch and galloped back towards the Hall.

I didn't hear the BMW drive into the yard, but I stopped work when I saw Leo looking up with a puzzled expression. I took off the walkman and watched the overdined Mr O'Rourke pick his way across the yard in his shiny brown shoes. He looked very dapper, in a

Sunday morning sort of way. Yet there was something that made his appearance stop short of being neat and tidy. I didn't pursue it – the dressing habits of old fogeys were not uppermost in my mind.

'Are your folks in, son?' he called out to Leo.

'Mam's in the kitchen' said Leo. 'Will I get her?'

'No, I know my way.' and he sidestepped the hens.

It must have been about twenty minutes later that he left. Aunt Brid was standing at the back door.

'Would you kids like a cup of tea?' she called.

'Great,' we said together. Anything to relieve this slave labour. We could see that she was worried.

'What is it, Mam?' asked Leo.

'Oh, nothing ...' she began. 'Oh heck, I have to tell *someone*. This O'Rourke fellow keeps pestering us to sell the place and I don't know what to do.' She fiddled with the biscuit crumbs on the table, making little roads with her finger.

'We're paying a mortgage on the house, plus the lease on the restaurant. Times are really tough, just at the moment. Now along comes O'Rourke making a great offer for the house. What he's offering would see us in luxury.' She stopped and sighed. 'But I love this place. It was derelict when we bought it and we've turned it into a lovely cottage. Well, I think it's lovely anyway.'

'Me too,' said Leo loyally. 'What will you do, Mam?'

Aunt Brid sighed again. 'Bloody money,' she said. 'I'll have to consider it; it's a very good offer. I know that, in the long run, the restaurant will make money. I really know that, but it will take a few years. The money he's offering – well we'd have it now.' She clasped her hands and twisted her fingers. 'But it would break my heart to leave here. There's more to life than money. Much more. I wish Jim had been here with me, I hate dealing with pushy people on my own.'

'I'm here,' said Leo rather forcefully. 'Talk to me about it. I'm in on this too, you know.'

Aunt Brid smiled at him. 'Of course you are, Leo. You know I'd do nothing without telling you. It's just that Jim is ...'

'Yeah. Jim's the big strong man and I'm just Leo the lad and you're just ... you're just a silly weak woman.' The chair scraped back as he got up and ran out. I got up to run after him and give him a good thump, but Aunt Brid put out a restraining hand.

'Leave him be, Maeve,' she said.

'The cheeky little prat,' I growled. 'How can you let him talk like that? He's a selfish pig.'

'It's all right,' she sighed and nodded. 'It's a long story, but Leo is going through a thorny patch in his relationship with Jim. It's a sort of no-win situation. If Jim tries to be friendly, Leo thinks he's trying to take his father's place. If Jim ignores him, Leo thinks it's because he resents him. I've tried reasoning with Leo, but ...' she shrugged her shoulders and shook her head.

'But Uncle Alec has been dead for years,' I put in. 'Sure Leo was only about four when he died. How can he remember ...? He's loved Jim all this time. Why the sudden change?'

Aunt Brid brushed the crumbs she'd been fiddling with into her hand and dropped them on to a plate. 'He found some photographs of himself and his father,' she continued 'They were taken when Leo was a toddler. Call it delayed grieving if you like, but I suppose it had to happen sooner or later. It's a phase and it will pass. We just have to tread gently.'

'I still don't see how you can let him ...' I began, not quite convinced.

'Just leave it be, Maeve. It will work out.'

'A good kick on the ...'

'Leave it be,' she said a bit more sharply. ('Keep your nose firmly on your own face, Maeve,' I warned myself.)

'Where would you go – if you sold out, I mean?' I asked, changing the subject.

She shook her head. 'I don't know. I just don't know what to think. We have to make up our minds by Wednesday week. The offer will be withdrawn then because, if we don't bite, he'll put the money into buying more land that's going up for sale on that day.' She got up. 'Anyway, I shouldn't be worrying you kids with my problems. Off you go and continue labouring in the fields.'

Later on, when we met Jamie, he handed me a small parcel of tinfoil. 'I thought you might like this,' he said.

It was a chicken sandwich. 'Oh, manna from heaven!' I cried. 'That is ...' I glanced at Leo. Better not make another foody joke. Not now. 'This is lovely. Here, Leo, have a bite.' I should have known better as he gave me a freaky look.

We sort of forgot about the abbey and its 'fecret chamber' over the next few days as the holidays took on a decidedly interesting pattern.

We got to meet old Mr McLaren on the second day. It was as we came back into the stable yard after riding in the paddock. By coincidence he was talking to O'Rourke.

They were deep in conversation. Jamie brought us over to introduce Leo and me.

Mr McLaren shook hands very formally. He was very tall and wore one of those quilted, sleeveless jackets over a thick sweater. He had a tweed cap on his head, like you see on those horsy types in photos of race-meetings. He had a grey moustache and nice eyes – for an old person.

'I'm delighted Jamie has found company,' he said. 'You're welcome here. Mr O'Rourke is trying to relieve me of my antiques,' he laughed by way of introducing O'Rourke.

'Yes, well he's good at ...' I stopped when Leo kicked me. So, I was mouthing off again, but I remembered the way that man had upset Aunt Brid and I wanted him to know he wasn't my flavour of the month.

O'Rourke nodded, his pink eyes sweeping over the three of us. 'I'll be off,' he said.

'You do that,' said Mr. McLaren, with a sort of polite barb. 'There are other ways of making money besides selling the ancestral artefacts, Mr. O'Rourke. But thank you for your interest.'

'What did that old geezer want from your grandfather?' I asked Jamie as we unsaddled the horses – at least as Jamie and Leo unsaddled the horses. For me, it was one thing to sit on the back of a horse, but nothing would induce me to venture anywhere near those hooves.

'Oh, he comes by now and then in the hope that grandad will sell him some of his antiques. He's persistent.'

I was about to tell Jamie about O'Rourke's visit to Aunt Brid, but, just at that moment, Fergus arrived to check that we'd put the nags away safely.

Over the next few days, Fergus continued to teach us better riding techniques. I continued to swoon whenever he helped me to board the big Daisy. I always pretended to have difficulty fastening the riding-helmet, so that I'd feel his fingers under my chin. Although I sometimes wondered if he could hear my heart thumping, it was worth that risk to get so close.

After a while the distance from the horse to the ground didn't seem quite so far and I wasn't at all panicked when Fergus suggested we take Daisy into the big field for a canter. He rode a classy mare even higher than Daisy, and Jamie rode his own horse. Leo and I took turns on Daisy. I wished that everyone I knew could see me as I rode with this magnificent creature. Fergus, that is. We

must have looked really cool as we trotted around the field on our high horses.

Several evenings later, after tea, Fergus gave Jamie driving-lessons in the Land Rover. 'Might as well start with something big,' he said.

I can't say the driving-lessons drove me wild with excitement; cars are a bore if you ask me. But I went along with the action anyway, just to be near Fergus. Leo, on the other hand, perched his skinny little body in the front with the other two and watched every move, asking questions about clutches and gears and thrilling things like that. I just feasted on Fergus's heart-stopping profile.

One night we went to the cinema in Kildioma. Fergus drove us in old McLaren's Merc. I thought at first he was coming too and I was glad I'd worn my new leggings and purple Docs, but he just gave us a cheery wave and zoomed off. I spent the rest of the night in a sweat of anxiety in case he'd gone on a date with some floozy. Now and then I squeezed my eyes shut and tried to use telepathy to make her (if there *was* a woman, that is) break out in ugly boils, scabby lips and swollen ankles.

We walked home afterwards and I insisted that we accompany Jamie through the back gate of the estate, just so that I could see if the lights were on in Fergus's place. He lived in a long apartment over the stables, which I thought was very romantic. The lights were out which did nothing for my morale. Tomorrow I would do my damnest to make him notice my feminine grace – I'd practise in front of the mirror tonight.

However, something occurred later which put my heavy charm-school plans on hold.

6

Something Suspicious at the Abbey

Later that night, when we were supposed to be in bed, we were messing about with Leo's computer in his room. The 'plink, plink' got on my nerves eventually and, besides, I wanted to practise my poses and expressions to make Fergus succumb to my feminine wiles tomorrow.

'Can't take a beating, Maeve?' Leo gloated.

'It's boring kid's stuff,' I retorted from the doorway. 'I'm going to bed.'

I had just got to the stage of saying 'prune' with delicately puckered lips when drowsiness hit me. I stretched out under the duvet and concentrated very hard on sending a telepathetic prune kiss across the fields to Fergus in his romantic flat above the stables.

Would Monarch be able to clear the high wall? Come on, Monarch, up! Oh damn, I mean, my goodness! The beautiful Miss Morris sailed through the air and crashed into unconsciousness. There was a different clatter of hooves as young Lord Chiselchin, also, by sheer coincidence, out on a lonely dawn gallop, happened on the scene.

'Miss Morris!' he cried, leaping from his horse, his heroically angelic face distraught with anxiety. 'Miss Morris! Maeve!'

'Maeve, will you wake up, you lazy deadbeat!'

'What?' Leo was shaking me.

'Those lights are at the abbey again.'

'Well so what?' I yawned. 'You said yourself that there was nothing we could do about those fellows lamping foxes.'

'Except that I don't think they're lamping foxes; the lights are too dim. I think it's someone up to no good.'

I looked at my watch. 'Leo, it's half past one. It's probably a courting couple who like to make out in weird places.'

'Courting couples don't have several torches shining all over the place. Come on, just have a look.'

'This is daft,' I said. But I put on my dressing-gown anyway and we tiptoed across to Leo's room.

'See, look.' He took a pile of books and a Jack Charlton poster off the window-seat so that we could see better. 'They're not the sort of lights used for lamping foxes. There's something going on. Do you think ... do you think maybe we should go over there and see what they're at?'

Sure enough, across the field there were indeed subdued lights twinkling in the vicinity of the abbey. However, Leo's suggestion that we make our way through the hostile dark and damp grass to see what was going on was really loopy.

'Are you out of your tiny excuse for a brain, Leo? It's half one and it's pitch-black. Anyway what could we do if it *is* someone up to no good? Clobber them with rolled-up newspapers and drag them to the garda station? Get real. I'm going back to bed.'

Leo looked at me scornfully. 'Chicken,' he said, flapping his arms and clucking. 'Afraid to go out in the dark.'

'I'm not scared. I just don't think ...'

'You are. You're scared.'

'Leave off, moron. I'm not in the least scared – neither of the dark nor those foxers or whatever they are.'

'Well, come on then. Come with me. I'm going anyway.'

I sighed. How could I get out of this without losing face? Leo saw that he'd won. 'We'll sneak out through the downstairs loo window – Ma and Jim would hear the door. Come on, get your wellies.'

His excitement got to me and, within minutes, we were hopping out on to the rockery under the loo.

Leo knew a short cut across the field to the abbey, thus avoiding the official track that tourists used. It was a starry night and our eyes got used to the dim light after a while. As we drew near to the abbey we could hear subdued voices. There was a truck parked outside the outer wall and three figures were lifting something heavy from it. My heart began to thump wildly – not a close-to-Fergus sort of thumping, more your average scared-to-death variety. These dudes were certainly doing something that was not politically correct. We crept as close as we dared, keeping outside the circle of light. The figures carried their burden into the abbey.

'Let's go before they come back,' I whispered to Leo. He shook his head, as I supposed the coward in me feared he would.

'Hold on for a while until we see what they're up to.'

The earthy smell of damp grass followed every breath through my nostrils (I kept my mouth closed against any night-stalking insects that might be shuffling about). My front felt cold and clammy as the dew found its way through my anorak and tee-shirt. I'd had enough; my patience was wearing thin. But before I could open my mouth to protest, the voices came within hearing distance again. Three male figures were silhouetted against the starry sky. One of them shone a torch around and we quickly ducked. The light briefly caught the other two. One of them seemed familiar. I racked my brains but I couldn't think where I'd seen him before.

'Let's get out of this place,' one of them said in a low voice. 'It gives me the creeps.'

'Me an' all,' agreed another voice, with a cockney sort of accent.

'Weirdsville.'

They hopped into the Range Rover and drove slowly to the end of the track without lights. Then they paused.

'I suppose they have someone posted as a look-out

down at the entrance,' said Leo. We watched as the truck gained speed and disappeared off towards the town.

'Let's take a look.' Leo pulled my arm as he headed for the outer wall.

'Might as well,' I agreed, before cowardice could override my curiosity.

Leo paused at the arch and peered at me in the dim light of the clear summer-night sky. 'Whatever it was, it was heavy enought to need three of them to carry it. Do you think ...' he swallowed. 'Do you think it might have been a body?'

The same thought had occurred to me, but I didn't want to dwell on it because I'd run screaming from the place.

'You make it sound like we're caught up in some kids' mystery story,' I scoffed with unconvincing bravado.

'What was it then?' persisted Leo.

'Arms,' I said.

'What?'

'Arms. It might be an arms dump for the IRA.'

'You and your IRA!' snorted Leo. 'They don't do that stuff any more.'

'It could be Middle-Eastern terrorists ...' I was not about to be put down so easily.

'Yeah, sure. They've come all this way to hide their guns here in ... in a ruin in a bog in Ireland! You're a nutter, Maeve.'

'Come on, let's have a look,' I said, just to show my superiority.

The suggestion didn't make much sense since neither of us had brought a torch. We groped about inside the ruined abbey – me with my heart in my mouth in case my hands might feel the cold sogginess of a dead person after all.

'Let's go,' I said eventually, with mature good sense. 'We'll come back tomorrow. Should we tell Jim ...?'

'No,' said Leo. 'Not Jim.'

I didn't push it – whatever was between Leo and Jim didn't need me muscling in on the scene.

'Your Ma?' I suggested.

'No,' said Leo again. 'She'd tell Jim. There'd be a fuss.'

'Maybe you're right,' I mused. 'Maybe it would only be a lot of fuss about nothing and we'd end up looking like a couple of eejits. We'll tell Jamie though. He'll be on our side.'

'OK,' agreed Leo. 'It'll be just the three of us then.'

Little did I think then what the consequences of that decision would be.

7

A Secret Revealed

'We think they're up to something fishy,' Leo said to Jamie next morning.

'Or drugs,' I added. 'It could be a store for drugs.'

Jamie listened with awe as we told him of our espionage the night before. In the light of day it seemed very adventurous and I was glad I'd been part of it.

'Once we saw the lights we knew something weird was going on, so we slipped across the field,' I said in a suitably low and dramatic tone of voice.

'Good for you,' said Jamie. I shot a warningly glittering glance at Leo; if he said one word about my not wanting to go at first, I'd – well, I'd make several moments of his life thoroughly uncomfortable. He got the message, smirked and said nothing. Power rests easy on me.

Jamie fidgetted with impatience. 'Come on,' he said. 'Let's go over and see if we can see anything now.'

'Shouldn't we tell Fergus?' I asked. 'He'd know what to do. Those prats could come back and catch us. They could be ruthless thugs – drug barons, Mafia even ...'

The others fell about. 'Mafia!' laughed Leo. 'There's no Mafia in Ireland.'

'The rain would wash them away,' put in Jamie.

'Well, anyway,' I said, 'they're up to no good, whoever they are, and I think we should tell Fergus.'

'I suppose so,' Jamie agreed reluctantly. 'I'd prefer to do this ourselves – once you bring adults in, the matter goes out of our hands. But you're probably right.'

I tried not to let the beam of pleasure shine through my face as I contemplated the joy of involving Fergus in our affairs. We made our way around to the stable yard. Reilly and a couple of grooms were saddling horses whose impatient hooves clip-clopped on the cobbles.

'Have you seen Fergus?' Jamie asked.

Reilly looked up and scowled. 'Land Rover's gone,' he growled. 'He ain't here.'

'That man really loves us,' I whispered to Jamie. I made a face at Reilly – mainly because I was cross that Fergus wasn't around.

Jamie laughed. 'Reilly's OK. He's been here so long he

thinks he owns the place. Don't mind him.' I looked up at the windows of the flat and hoped that Fergus might be there. Languishing. Thinking of me.

'Try the flat,' I said to Jamie.

He shrugged his shoulders. 'If the Land Rover's gone ...' he began.

'Your grandad might have it,' I hoped I didn't sound desperate. 'Let's just try.'

'All right.' Jamie led the way up the stone steps to Fergus's door. I let my hand rest on the old-fashioned brass doorknocker and held my breath as I gently rapped. 'Please let him be inside and glad to see us – to see me,' I prayed. But, when the second knock brought no response, I had to swallow my disappointment.

'Perhaps he's in the paddock,' I said.

'No. He's gone somewhere in the Land Rover.' Jamie was emphatic and getting more impatient. 'We're wasting time. Let's go.'

The beautiful Miss Morris tried to warn Lord Chiselchin of the goings-on of his housekeeper and her scumbag nephew, but in her weak state the words wouldn't come out. She fainted again. Her handsome rescuer picked her up gently and carried her towards Darkling Hall, which stood silhouetted against the early morning mist. Up the imposing staircase he rushed and laid the beautiful Miss Morris on her attic bed. He patted her porcelain hand. Her eyelashes fluttered.

'What happened?' she asked. Then she saw the concerned face above her.

'I must warn ...' she began.

'It's all right, your lordship,' a sharper voice cut across her. 'I'll look after the young lady now.'

The beautiful Miss Morris paled as Pickaxe bustled into the room. Where had she come from? She seemed to simply materialise behind his lordship. How had she got here so quickly, and were those cobwebs in her hair, or did she simply use cheap shampoo?

'Leave her to me,' she continued, her yellow teeth bared. 'I'll see to her every comfort. McHayseed is waiting to take you to the station. And your uncle, Lord Grabgreed, has come to look after things while you're away. Don't you worry about a thing; Miss Morris will be back with your young ward Edward in no time at all.'

'You're so kind, Pickaxe,' smiled Lord Chiselchin. He glanced around the dismal attic and a frown creased his marble brow. 'Move her into the Pink Room. This place is quite dreary.'

The beautiful Miss Morris clutched at his hand and tried desperately to speak, but he just put his finger on her lips and said, 'There, there, my dear. Don't stress yourself. Pickaxe will look after you.'

Pickaxe's face twisted into an evil grin. 'Indeed,' she sneered.

'Bloody h ... I mean alas,' thought the beautiful Miss Morris as Lord Chiselchin's broad back disappeared out through the door.

'What's with the long face?'

'What?'

Jamie was looking at me as we made our way through the hole in the wall.

'I said, what's with the long face. You look like someone took your lollipop.'

'Just thinking,' I muttered.

'Thinking that the Mafia are lying in wait for us at the abbey,' laughed Leo. 'She imagines that they're going to put concrete boots on us and toss us into the river.'

'Give over,' I snarled as Fergus's face melted from my thoughts. 'You watch too much rubbish. Anyway,' I couldn't resist a barb, 'if you were nicer to Jim your home wouldn't be so full of tension.'

Leo's face froze and he stopped.

'What to you mean by that?'

I could see that I'd gone a tad too far, but you can't rub out words once they're said.

I swallowed. 'Well you're pretty rude to Jim and he works bloomin' hard. He deserves a bit more than bad-mouthing from you. It upsets your ma too. Anyone can see that. They've enough to worry about without you giving them extra hassle.'

'That's none of your business,' Leo gritted. 'Don't stick your nose in where it's not wanted.'

'He's very fond of you, Jim is,' I protested. 'Can't you see that?'

'Ha! Like hell he is. Jim thinks only of my ma and Miriam – they're his family. I'm just someone who ...'

'Oh yeah. Do the poor little martyr now,' I snapped. 'Jim's been a father to you since he married your ma three years ago. All of a sudden you want to be pitied.'

'He's *not* my father!'

'Excuse me.' Jamie put himself between Leo and me. 'Are we going to the abbey or do you two want to drop the idea and continue with your family squabble? If so I'm going home.'

'It's all right,' I said, glaring at Leo. 'We're finished.'

'Finished is right,' spat Leo. ' I don't care if I never see you again. You're … you're a rude and selfish cow who can't mind her own business.'

'It *is* my business. Your ma is my aunt – my favourite aunt. I hate to see a little prig like you make her miserable. And Jim too. I like Jim.'

Jamie looked at both of us with an awkward and fed-up expression, nodded, and headed back the way we'd come.

'Now look at what you've done,' I hissed at Leo.

'Me? You're the one …'

'Jamie!' I called. 'Come on, it's OK.'

Jamie turned. 'I'd hate to intrude on a family row. Fight it out between you, but don't ask me to stand about and listen, thank you very much.'

'It's nothing.' I tried to laugh nonchalantly, but it came out like a squeak. 'Please come back.'

Leo was standing still, white-faced. Jamie reached over and patted his shoulder. Nothing was said, but the momentary intimacy seemed to shut me out and I felt strangely isolated. Still, I wasn't sorry for what I'd said. I tossed my head and led the way towards the abbey.

It looked very harmless and one could scarcely believe that there had been weird business going on there the night before. By the time the others caught up I was back to my normal, intelligently capable self.

'I was thinking,' Jamie was saying, 'about the secret chamber. I was thinking about it last night.'

'Yes?' I prompted.

'Well, we'd been thinking in terms of something that clicks open; something mechanical. But in the eleventh or twelfth centuries they wouldn't have been that sophisticated.'

'True,' agreed Leo. As if he'd know.

'So,' continued Jamie, 'it has to be something simple, like a raised carving which acts like a latch.'

'That's clever,' said Leo.

'Clever of me or clever of the monks?' laughed Jamie.

I was a bit relieved to see Leo laughing too. He looked around the ruined nave and passed into the inner chamber, called the abbot's quarters.

'That proves it,' he called from inside the latter.

'Proves what?' Jamie made his way across.

'That there *is* a secret chamber. Where else could they have put that heavy load they were carrying? We'd have seen them if they came back today and there's no sign of the bod ... of the yoke they took from the truck. So they *must* have put it somewhere secret.'

'I knew we'd be coming here today,' said Jamie. 'Even though I didn't know of the goings-on last night, I'd been thinking about the abbey and intended that we come here. I even put a torch in my pocket. In case we might strike lucky,' he added. 'So let's start looking.'

The chancel and the nave were laid with the original flagstones. In recent years these had been covered with a layer of fine pebbles, I suppose to stop moss and stuff. I went and fetched a lumpy rock.

'And what are you going to do with that?' asked Leo. 'Break holes in the ground?'

Could he never leave it alone? I gritted my teeth.

'What I'm going to do, Mr Smartypants, is to tap the flags for a hollow sound.'

'Good thinking,' said Jamie. The way he said it made the word 'gentleman' flash into my mind. In another era, Jamie would have ended up as owner of a large country estate making peace among the warring peasants – or is it pheasants? I can never remember which is which; living in a city one doesn't have much to do with either. I tap-tapped with my stone. There it was – a hollow sound!

'Bingo,' said Jamie. 'Now all we have to do is find the entrance.'

There were several rose-type carvings around the floor of the chancel which we hadn't noticed before as they were covered by pebbles. We took an area each and tried turning the carvings this way and that.

'Gotcha!' Leo exulted eventually. 'Look! This turns like a door handle. I found it!'

Sure enough, the rose carving turned quite easily and there was a gentle click.

'That must mean that it's unlocked,' Jamie said in almost a whisper.

We stood for a moment, not quite knowing what to do next. My father once said that our journey through life depends on which of the many twists and turns in the pathways we choose to follow. I'd never quite understood what he meant until now. Did I really want to follow this path? If I discovered something unspeakably evil here would it change my life forever? Before I had time for further deeply philosophical thought, Jamie and Leo were puffing and panting as they tried to raise the flagstone.

'Come on, Maeve,' gasped Jamie. 'Grab hold and give us a hand.'

I sighed and dug my fingers under the rim. Gradually the stone began to move and a gaping hole was revealed. The smell of damp and decay that emanated from its black depths was pukey. Well-worn steps led down into the dark pit. The trees around the abbey swished in a

sudden breeze, lending an eeriness to the surreal atmosphere.

'I suppose we'd better go down,' said Jamie. 'Now that we've got this far, we might as well go the whole hog.'

'I don't know,' I began. Thoughts of descending into that hole, where God knew what kind of living or dead things waited, scared me witless. 'What if those fellows come back?'

'They won't.' Leo was excited. 'Sure didn't they leave their stuff here last night – in the dark. They're hardly going to come back in daylight and take it away.'

'All right,' I conceded. 'You two go first.'

It was dark and very smelly going down those steps and I hated what I was doing. 'What did those daft monks want to dig a hole under their monastery for anyway?' I grumbled.

'Protection against the Vikings,' Jamie's voice was muffled as from a distance. 'The Vikings came down the Shannon river, plundering the monastic settlements and taking valuable church ornaments.'

'Where did they get them?' asked Leo. 'The church ornaments, I mean. Where did the monks get them?'

'They made them,' Jamie's voice seemed farther away now, as if he'd passed under an arch or something. 'Ireland was once very rich in gold. Christianity came very peacefully into Ireland in the fifth century and the monks just continued with the same style of art that the Celts had been using for years, only they used it in things like chalices and shrines for saints' bones and stuff like that.'

'And the Vikings got wind of these and nicked them?' asked Leo.

'I thought they built round towers against those invasions,' I called after them. I hadn't fallen asleep during *every* history class.

'Well, these boys seem to have gone down rather than up to protect their bits and pieces,' said Jamie. 'Anyway, here we are.'

He flashed his torch around. We, me bringing up the rear, were in a small chamber, about the size of Aunt Brid's kitchen. It was like something from a creepy film, except that we weren't sitting in a cinema stuffing ourselves with popcorn; we were *in* it and this was for real.

8

The Hoard

Stacked all around the walls were hunks of stone, some covered with sacking which gave them an eerie look, like wrapped corpses. They had carvings on them.

'Cripes!' we all seemed to exclaim together. So this was the secret stash cloaked in the secrecy of midnight intrigue.

'Some of these are Christian and some are pre-Christian,' Jamie whistled. Having listened to his fancy lecture coming down the stairs, I was getting slightly peed off with his spewing out these gems of knee-trembling facts. It bothered me that Jamie seemed to know so much. But then, I consoled myself, he was, after all, pushing fourteen.

'How did you know about ... about all this stuff?' I gestured around the chamber. 'Dreary old facts. You'd be better off knowing something important, like how to ride a Harley-Davison or how to make up rap songs ...'

'Maeve!' Leo snapped. 'You just hate anyone to know more than you, don't you? Which means you must hate an awful lot of people because you don't know nothing.'

'That's a double negative,' I said triumphantly. 'It means I know everything.'

'Drop dead,' muttered Leo.

'It's all right, Leo,' Jamie shone the torch on Leo's angry face. 'I probably do go on a bit. My Irish granny has a degree in art history – she writes books about Celtic times and all that. I'm ... I've always had a bit of an interest I suppose. You pick up things when you spend a lot of time with someone who has a special interest.'

Indeed! Here was I knowing all about the working parts of a horse because I, well we, were spending a lot of time with Fergus.

'Is that the granny who's gone off with the Norwegian fisherman?' I asked. Jamie nodded. Well, at least she had some redeeming aspects in her favour.

'Are we going to look at this stuff or not?' Leo asked impatiently. 'We don't want to be down here too long.'

'Right on,' agreed Jamie.

He shone the torch on individual items. They were mostly stonework – round things with hollows in the middle which Jamie said were querns that were used for grinding corn, other rounded stones with sort of honey-

suckle patterns carved on them, slabs with crosses and little square men incised rather than carved, and bits of what seemed to be arches with worn faces on them. There were also chalices and other churchy stuff which Jamie said were silver, but to me they looked like scrap tin.

'Polished up, these would fetch a fortune,' he said.

'I'll take you word for it,' I said doubtfully. 'Looks like a load of junk to me.'

'Why would anyone stash a load of junk in a secret place like this?' asked Leo. He had a point, but I pretended not to hear.

'I said ...' he persisted.

'I know. I heard you the first time ... What do we do now?' I turned towards Jamie.

'Tell the gardai,' put in Leo. 'Tell them pronto. We don't want to hang around here.'

'I don't know ...' began Jamie doubtfully.

'What don't you know?' I asked, for once siding with my cousin. 'I think that's what we ought to do. Why should you have a problem with that, Jamie?'

'No problem,' said Jamie. 'It's just ... oh, you're right. Let's do that.'

'Should we bring something?' I asked, reaching for a chalice. 'Just to prove that we're not making this up?' As I picked it up, something small clattered from underneath. Jamie shone the torch on it. It was another of those buttons with a yacht on it. So now we had two droopy-drawered monks from way back when.

'What was that?' asked Jamie.

'Just an old button,' I said dismissively. 'Maybe we should wrap this chalice in something so that we're not parading through the town with it.'

'Here,' said Leo, taking off his sweater. 'I'm too hot anyway. Wrap it in this.'

'I wish we had found Fergus that time,' I said as I wound the sweater around the chalice. 'If he was here now, he'd know what to do.'

'He'd do what we're doing now,' said Leo. 'Go to the garda station. What else is there to do? Come on, we'll take a short-cut through old ... through Jamie's grandad's place and get out on to the main road. At least it'll be quicker.'

We carefully replaced the flagstone and shuffled about on the pebbles to spread them around. The place looked as harmless and peaceful as ever.

The beautiful Miss Morris raised herself painfully on an elbow when she saw the lights from outside flickering on the high ceiling of the darkening room. How could she have been asleep since early morning? Then she remembered the tea which one of the maids had brought. No wonder it tasted funny – it must have been drugged!

Hearing footsteps coming along the corridor, Miss Morris closed her eyes and pretended to be asleep. The door opened quietly. Squinting through her long, curly lashes, the beautiful Miss Morris saw Pickaxe enter, carrying a lantern which highlighted her sharp, cruel face. There was somebody with her. It was an old geez ... an elderly gentleman.

'Are you sure she's unconscious?' he asked.

Pickaxe's mouth twisted into a satisfied smirk. 'Of course, your lordship. Didn't I make up the potion myself? She'll be out for hours yet.'

Your lordship! Miss Morris almost gave the game away by

gasping aloud. Who was this nasty person? Then she remembered Pickaxe's words to Lord Chiselchin. "Your uncle, Lord Grabgreed, is here," she had said. The uncle was up to no good!

'*Good,' he said. 'Let's get back to the others then, my dear. After tonight, all of this will be ours. Did you make sure to leave plenty of evidence so that my goody-goody cousin will get the blame?'*

'*Of course,' smiled Pickaxe. 'Didn't I succeed with his younger brother? Soon they will both be languishing in jail. Nothing can stop us now.'*

'*I shall be master and you shall be mistress of Darkling Hall,' went on the man. 'Come along, my dear. We mustn't delay.'*

The beautiful Miss Morris gasped when they'd left. So this crummy uncle was planning to take Darkling Hall from its owner and install Pickaxe as its mistress. Perish the thought!

She crossed the carpeted floor to the huge bay window and drew back the heavy curtains. Down below, on the navy-blue, rolling lawn, a line of dark-cloaked people carrying lanterns were furtively making their way in the direction of the cliffs which dotted the east side of the estate. Miss Morris's eyes scanned ahead to try and make out where they were going.

Beyond the beautiful gardens and the moors and the cliffs lay the sea. The line of lights was heading right at the ruined chapel beyond the lawn. Skull Cove! They were heading for Skull Cave and not the place where she had espied them this morning. Why? Had they more treasure stashed there? She opened the window and leaned out. The wind from the sea carried the voices to her delicate ears.

'*Move along. Quickly! This stuff must be moved before dawn,' shouted a gruff voice she recognised as belonging to*

Lord Grabgreed.

There was a small dot on the horizon, just visible in the diminishing twilight. The beautiful Miss Morris screwed up her eyes to see better. It was a ship. Then she remembered; two days ago while she was in town buying stuff – buying books for young Edward, she'd heard a seafaring man mention that a Spanish ship would be passing with a consignment of ...'

'What's gold bullion?' I asked as we crossed the field. Leo looked at me with a puzzled expression.

'It's gold or silver ingots.'

'Ingots?'

'Sort of bars. It's like ... like raw gold or silver. Before it's made into something it comes in bars.'

'So it's very valuable?'

'Yes it is,' added Jamie. 'But why are you asking? There's no gold or silver bullion back there.'

'I know, I know, just wondering.'

Leo grinned. 'Don't mind her,' he said. 'She's always coming out with daft thoughts. For Pete's sake don't go telling the gardai that there's gold bullion under the abbey.'

I snorted and resumed swishing through the long grass towards the hole in the wall.

Gold! So, why were these people heading towards Skull Cove? Suddenly Miss Morris froze as realisation dawned on her. These toerags – these evil people were wreckers! They were on their way to shine their lights on Skull Cove to trick the unfortunate Spaniards into thinking that it was the harbour. The Spaniards would set their course towards the false lights, flounder on the rocks, and the crooked Pickaxe and her

*cohorts would salvage the gold. And dear Lord Chiselchin was
to get the blame!*

*The beautiful Miss Morris swept towards the door.
Something must be done to stop that rotten lot! But in vain
did she turn the handle of the door. It was firmly locked. She
pounded desperately on the heavy oak door, but the sound
echoed hollowly in the empty house. Was there not one single
good person on the whole estate to hear her cries and help save
the poor Spaniards from the wreckers? 'Lord Chiselchin,' she
sobbed as she sank to the floor. 'Oh, Lord Chiselchin, please
come home.'*

As we passed around by the conservatory, I saw the
Land Rover come up the front avenue and swing in
towards the arch leading to the stable yard.

'It's Fergus!' I exclaimed. 'Look, he's back. Come on,
let's tell him about our find.'

The other two stopped and looked back at me. They
didn't share my enthusiasm. But then, the god of love
had not shot either of them through the heart with a red-
hot arrow. 'At least he might give us a lift to the garda
station,' I added with great conviction.

'I suppose ...' began Leo.

Jamie shook his head. 'Let's leave it, Maeve. Let's just
keep it to ourselves ...'

'No!' I was wasn't going to lose this chance. 'Come on.'

They followed me around to the stables. My pounding
heart stopped beating and sank into my stomach when I
saw that the yard was empty. The Land Rover, still warm
from *his* touch, was parked beneath the stone steps.

'Too late,' said Jamie. 'He could be anywhere. Let's
go.'

We turned back towards the arch. Suddenly a voice from above called out, 'Hey, you lot. Looking for me?'

'Fergus!' I cried. He was standing outside his door, Romeo in Levis. 'We've something terribly important to tell you.'

'In that case you'd better come on up,' he replied.

'Come on up!' The words were magic. Was I about to see the intimate surroundings of God's hunkiest creation? Would I be able for this without conking out on the floor in a glorious swoon? Fergus held the door open as I bounded up the stone steps, the others trailing along behind.

'What's so important?' he laughed.

I dramatically unwrapped the chalice and held it out

for him to see. His expression changed to dismay – which was very gratifying and made me feel very mature indeed. He glanced quickly around the yard and ushered us into his flat. It was everything I'd imagined it to be. There was a comfortable easy chair in front of an old-fashioned range. Books and magazines lay scattered on a pine table. Some empty beer bottles lay in a waste-paper bin; I forgave him for that – he was probably lonely and sought refuge in beer. I'd soon sort that out when he found out he was in love with me. An antique dresser bore further signs of his endearing bachelorhood; letters lay in an untidy heap, a mug with 'I've been to Dublinia' written on it was full of pencils and biros.

Beside a radio with two big speakers were stacks of tapes and CDs. Straining my neck, I could make out U2, Elton John and Meatloaf. Old stuff, but then Fergus was a man in his twenties.

He was running his big, capable hero's hands gently over the surface of the chalice.

'Tell me where you found this,' he said in a low, even voice.

We told him about the manuscript and its mention of the secret chamber and how we didn't believe it until the night Leo and I had seen the action at the abbey.

'I felt we had to see what was going on,' I said. 'When we saw the lights.'

'And this is the sort of thing they have stored down there,' Leo put in, breathlessly. 'You should see it, Fergus. They have stuff nicked from all sorts of places you'd read about in history books.'

'And you came straight here?' said Fergus. 'I'm touched.'

'Yes,' I replied, bursting with pride. 'We wanted you to be the first to know. I said all along, didn't I, that we must tell you. That you'd know what to do. It's lucky you were here. I'm ... I'm really glad.'

Fergus looked at me and I gave him a knowing smile. At least I thought it was a knowing smile, but Fergus didn't seem to know. He got up and went to the window, still holding the chalice.

'Don't you think we should tell your grandad, Jamie?' he said after a few moments. 'After all the abbey is on his land. He has a right to know.'

Jamie shook his head. 'No, he'd only create a mega fuss. Besides, he's not here. He's gone to a race-meeting in Tralee with Reilly.' His face suddenly registered surprise. 'I thought you knew that. Had you forgotten? I'm sure I heard him tell you yesterday evening ...'

Fergus slapped his forehead. 'Of course. Yes, I had forgotten.'

'Will you come with us, Fergus?' I asked. 'Give us a lift? Though it's not just for the lift that we want you to come ... Like I said, we really want you to be in on this. Part of the deal ... so it's not just for the lift. We can walk if you like ...' I hate it when I get flustered – my words get all tangled up and my face goes red. But Fergus smiled and looked out of the window again.

'Our secret, is it?'

'Yeah,' said Leo. 'We'll probably get our photos in the paper.'

'OK, then,' said Fergus. 'Our secret it will be. Let's slip away to town and not tell a soul ...'

'Until we get to the cop shop,' I finished. Fergus nodded and smiled just at me.

'As you say, until we get to the cop shop,' he agreed. He went to the door and looked around the yard. It was still empty. 'Right,' he went on. 'You folks get into the back of the Land Rover, and stay out of sight.'

'Why?' asked Leo. 'Why should we stay out of sight?'

'Because,' explained Fergus patiently. "You'd never know; those guys might have seen you coming out. You were so excited about your find that you probably dashed back here without checking to see if there was anyone about. They could have followed you here and might be lying in wait. If they saw you in the Land Rover they'd know what we're up to and ram us or something. We'd be no match for a bunch like that …the grooms who didn't travel with your grandad are all out on the track. There's nobody around except us.'

'Why don't we ring the gardai and let them come here?' asked Jamie.

Fergus shook his head. 'Those thugs could be around here right now and do fair damage before the gardai would arrive. The sooner we move away from here the better. Come on. Quick.'

9

Shattered Dreams

We took the steps two at a time and bundled into the back of the Land Rover. Fergus hopped in and, with a grim look on his wonderful profile, gunned the engine into action. We tore down the long, tree-lined avenue and screeched to a halt at the big iron gates.

'Any sign of anyone suspicious?' Leo asked. You could see he was enjoying this cloak-and-dagger stuff. I suppose we were all enjoying it now that Fergus was in charge.

Fergus looked both ways and shook his head. I glanced at Jamie. He had a very worried look on his face. And I mean seriously worried. Suddenly the scales fell from my eyes! His grandad must be involved in this crime. The abbey was on his land and he had the original book about the place. Also, he was finding it hard to keep up the grand house and all that. He needed more dosh – Jamie himself had said so. No wonder Jamie had seemed so reluctant to share our secret. His old grandad was a crook!

I felt sorry for him but he'd have to learn that crime does not pay. So what if the old man ended up in the slammer, good enough for him trying to flog chunks of our heritage to foreigners. And that miserable Reilly – he was in on the act too and resented having Fergus around in case himself and the crooked Mr McLaren would be found out. They probably used the innocent front of going around to race-meetings as a cover for their evil activities. Probably stuffed the stolen carvings and things

into the horse-boxes. Why didn't I think of this before?

I breathed on the chalice and tried to polish it with the sleeve of my sweater. I wanted to impress the gardai with our find and not have them think that we were getting excited about a pre-Christian lager can. When the breathing didn't work, I tried spit, but that didn't work either. I stuck it back in Leo's sweater and consoled myself with admiring the beautiful scenery – Fergus's face in the mirror, that is.

I glanced at Jamie again. His face was still white and tense. I wouldn't break the news to him yet that I had sussed the situation and knew his grandad was a conman. Fergus would know how to handle it and I would be on hand to console poor Jamie.

'I'm just going to call to a mate of mine,' Fergus called back to us. 'He knows all there is to know about antiques and things. I'd like to show him the chalice, if you don't mind. You can also tell him about the other stuff under the abbey and he'll be able to give you a fair idea of what it is and where it has come from. Information that'll help them when we get to the garda station. OK?'

Leo looked at Jamie, who simply nodded. 'If you like,' he said.

I didn't want anyone else muscling in on our act. There were bound to be interviews and things and four faces are enough on any front-page photo – any more constitutes a crowd, thus diluting the fame. I opened my mouth to argue and Fergus caught my eye in the mirror. He winked and I melted. Besides, he was a Perfect Being and who was I to argue with his logic? We turned off a side road before the town and travelled for a couple of miles. As we passed through a pair of high gates I glanced at Leo and raised my eyebrows questioningly. He shrugged and shook his head. Fat lot he knew of his environs.

Fergus pulled up at a big shed and turned to us. 'I'll just go and get Dave,' he said. 'You're safe here – don't get out.'

We watched him disappear into the shed.

I looked again at Jamie's face. He was not a happy person.

'Jamie,' I began. It was showdown time. 'I know about your grandfather.' (I used the formal term because of the seriousness of the situation.) 'I think you're very brave to try and hold out on his behalf, but his time has come ...'

Jamie frowned. 'What are you on about?' he asked.

'Your grandad. It's your grandad, isn't it? Your grandad and old Reilly are nicking stuff and selling it? Don't be ashamed. It's not your fault and we'll say that you knew nothing about it ...'

'Here's Fergus,' Leo called out with relief. 'Look.'

Sure enough Fergus was coming out of the shed, followed by another man. And another, and another.

'Jeez, he's told the whole world!' gasped Leo. 'What's he thinking?'

'Plain clothes cops!' I exclaimed. 'They've been staking out the place and are moving in to make an arrest. Don't panic, Jamie. We'll look after you.'

Then I recognised one of the men.

'Hell!' I clutched at Leo's arm. 'That fellow who's just behind Fergus ...'

'It's one of the guys who was at the abbey last night!' put in Leo.

'And the other day,' I added. 'He's the one who was at

the abbey the first day we went there.'

I felt a panic begin to rise in my throat. Plain clothes cops don't do shady things in old ruins at night. This was getting pretty heavy. But Fergus was there, so everything must be OK.

The group approached the Land Rover very swiftly. I frantically searched Fergus's face for some sign that everything was cool, that these were really nice people out to help us. But his face was white and strange.

Menacing. One of the men opened the door. Two of them went around to the other door.

'Just get out and you'll be all right,' said Fergus. 'Don't try any heroics.'

I tried to swallow, but there was no spit in my mouth.

'Fergus ...?' I began.

He looked at me grimly and I was far more scared of his face than I was of the other thugs. This man who had been such fun for us and who had taught us riding had coldly switched out the light of friendship and replaced it with chilling indifference.

10

Things Get Out of Hand

The three of us just stood for a moment, numb and dumb, as we stared at the hostile faces around us.

'What's happening, Fergus?' Jamie asked at last. 'What's the pitch?'

'The pitch, Mister Muck, is that you lot are causing us a right pain in the neck.' One of the men leaned threateningly towards Jamie. 'Years of bloody work snuffed out because you baskets have nothing better to do than poke about where you've no business. I've half a mind to ...'

'Shut it, Ber.' Fergus put out a restraining hand. 'That wouldn't help. If we work it out reasonably, no one gets hurt, no one gets caught and the deal goes ahead as planned.'

'Yeah,' spat Ber, his thick neck strained with anger and his fat nostrils quivering. He was wearing a grubby tee-shirt with 'Féile 94' written in faded letters across the tight chest. 'A million-pound deal up in smoke.'

'I said, "Shut it!"' Fergus turned on him. 'Nothing's gone up in smoke. And it won't. The deal will go through and we'll be far away before anyone's the wiser.' He nodded grimly at the three of us. 'You folks just do what you're told and you'll be OK. Now, nice and easy, go into that shed.'

Jamie never took his eyes off Fergus. 'My grandad trusted you, Fergus. We all did.'

Fergus nodded and shrugged his shoulders. 'That's

life, son. He was meant to trust me. Now move.'

'No,' Leo piped up. 'Buzz off, scumbags.'

'Better do as they say,' Jamie said in a low voice.

Wimp, I thought. Trust him, with his uppity ways, to give in so easily.

'Like hell,' uttered Leo and he dived between two of the men and scarpered down the avenue.

'Damn! Get him,' ordered Fergus. Ber and the fellow called Dave, who we'd seen at the abbey, raced after the little skinny figure of Leo. 'Don't try that,' Fergus turned to Jamie and me. 'It's not worth broken bones,' he added ominously. I glanced at his face to see if there was any sign of friendship, that he would smile and say it was just a joke and we'd all continue on to the garda station. But he just kept us locked in an icily menacing stare.

There were shouts and screams as Leo was dragged back. To give the little reptile his due, he was putting up a good fight and made it hard going for the two thugs to subdue his flailing legs and arms as they carried him. He caught Ber a neat kick just below his 'Féile 94'. Ber drew out with his open palm and smacked Leo right on the side of his head. Beside me I could sense Jamie bristling.

'Thick gorilla!' he swore, his genteel hormones doing an about-turn. He leapt towards the struggling trio and laid into Ber with both fists. Fergus and the remaining two fellows joined the fray. I stood with hypnotic awe and watched the metamorphosis of Jamie, from a refined member of the Good China Used Every Day class, into a raging bull.

Standing? What was I doing standing there when my brave companions were having at a bunch of ... of gorillas. I looked at Fergus, my heroically, angelically handsome

Perfect Being, my mega heart-throb, the love of my life, my own Lord Chiselchin. Then I took the chalice from its wrapping and thumped his marble brow with it.

'Bitch,' he snarled, and knocked me to the ground.

'Only a thug like you would strike a lady,' gasped Jamie, his nose dripping blood.

A lady! As I sat in a crumpled heap on the ground in the middle of this unreal, violent scene, all I could focus my mind on was the fact that Jamie had called me a lady.

The fight was over in seconds and the three of us were bundled into the shed. Though we had lost, it was satisfying to see the panting boyos nursing scratch marks and kicked shins. We knew there was little point in trying to make a run for it. I gave Jamie a ragged tissue to try and staunch the flow of blood from his nose. It wasn't much help, and bits of the tissue stuck to the congealing blood, giving him the appearance of someone in a grisly movie.

'What now?' asked Dave, sucking a grazed knuckle. 'We can't let the blighters go.'

'Well of course we can't,' snapped Ber. 'If I'd my way, I'd ...'

'We all know what you'd do if you had your way.' Fergus was rooting about among some bales of hay. 'And you'd have us doing time for GBH or worse.'

Worse? I tried to swallow. This was not happening. This was kids' storybook stuff with added violence and bad language. But the bruise on my arm told me that it was painfully for real.

'Mossy, go and ring Stephen. Tell him we'll have to move the consignment before the deadline. And tell him about these interfering kids. We need to talk, to decide on what to do.'

'Me tell him?' the fourth man, Mossy, exclaimed. He was what my mother would call a stocky man – big shoulders and body supported by legs that seemed to curve outwards to bear the weight. Bandy, I think, is the word. He had a beard and, in different circumstances, I'd have rated his looks as pretty cool. Except for the legs.

'Jeez, Fergus, he'll blow a gasket. Why can't someone else ...?'

'Just do it. Stop whining and get it done. Every second we waste is dangerous. Someone will start looking for this lot sooner or later and the place will be crawling with boys in blue. Tell Stephen to get here without delay. Go on, get your ass moving.'

Mossy shuffled out, muttering to himself. There was no doubt that we were causing a lot of hassle. The way that they were snapping at one another was evidence enough that we'd upset them more than just a tad.

'Give me a hand to tie these kids up,' Fergus said.

'Hey!' I protested. 'There's no need for that.'

'Shut up,' grunted Ber. I shut up; you don't argue with a huffy gorilla in a 'Féile 94' tee-shirt.

With business-like efficiency, the other two swiftly tied us with the baler twine that Fergus had been rooting for. Then they began to build a wall of hay bales around us. I must confess I panicked at this stage. Up to now I'd been too busy being angry to entertain thoughts of being afraid. But now the situation had got heavy and I felt the nightmare chill of real fear at the nape of my neck.

How long were they going to leave us here? Would we be found in a hundred years' time, three skeletons bound together with baler twine, while the great-great-grandchildren of these scum pranced about on the Costa Lotsa with the money from whatever deal was going on now.

I felt tears of frustration pricking my eyes. Any second now and I'd be a blubbering mess. Leo looked at me, his eyes wide with fear. His lower lip went into a down curve and tears coursed a track through the grime on his face.

'Oh God, Maeve, what will we do?' His whisper was broken with sobs. 'I'm scared.'

Something in me snapped and checked my own tears; this terrified little boy was searching for any shred of hope I might offer and, by jingo, I was not about to let him down. I twisted slightly until my hand found his and I squeezed it hard.

'Don't worry,' I whispered. 'They can't do anything to us. We'll be out of here soon. Just be patient.'

How long could I keep up a brave front before that chilling fear would grip my neck again? Anger – that was the answer. If I could stay angry it would keep the fear at bay.

The beautiful Miss Morris got up from her knees. Suddenly she felt very angry. Angry at the mob who cared nothing for the lives of the sailors they were about to condemn to the waves. She stood erect, her delicate nostrils flared with wrath. The all-consuming anger fired her with resolution; she would prevent this evil deed or ... or die in the attempt.

Anger! I'd got to stay angry. I gave Leo's hand another reassuring squeeze.

'Should we gag them?' asked Dave. Fergus shook his head.

'Who'd hear them here? Anyway they're going to be co-operative little kids and do what we tell them, aren't you, lads.'

'Lads! I'm not a lad,' I growled. It wasn't important. It was just an excuse for me to show him how much I hated him.

'We can see that,' slobbered Ber. He reached over and stroked my hair. I recoiled in horror, sorry I'd opened my big mouth.

'You leave her alone,' said Jamie.

Ber's leer turned to an ugly grimace and he raised his hand to strike Jamie. I longed for the good old days when gangsters didn't swing punches at kidnappees. Not in any of the old films I've seen on satellite.

'Cop yourself on, Ber,' put in Dave. 'Things are getting under control, so don't mess.'

'Yah!' Ber growled at Jamie. Still, it was a relief when he moved away. They piled a few more bales of hay so

that we were now surrounded on all sides. We sat, tense and shocked, as the voices faded. The heavy doors swung shut with a jarring note of doom. Part of me wanted those nerds to stay – at last the sound of human speech, however threatening, was better than the silence of not knowing what was ahead of us. Another part of me wanted them to be as far away as possible. Let them do their cruddy deals with their lumps of rock and dreary, dented metal things and let us get back to a life I would never take for granted ever again. Never. Honest. One word of complaint would never make its way past my lips if I could just get my normal life back.

Of course we immediately set about trying to loosen the twine, but the efforts only made it bite deeper into our skin.

'No good,' muttered Jamie. 'Those knots are for keeps.

The creeps must be ex-boy-scouts,' he added wryly.

'I want to get away,' Leo's voice was shaking. 'I *have* to get away.'

'Have you an urgent appointment, Leo?' I snorted, to my shame forgetting my earlier vow of minding the kid. Old habits die hard even when your world is suddenly going down the plug-hole. 'Please don't let us keep you.'

'Listen,' Jamie's voice was full of authority. 'We're probably going to be left like this for a while. It's vital that we co-operate – that we look out for one another. Know what I mean? If we start squabbling among ourselves and jigging about selfishly, then we're lost altogether. We've got to stay calm. OK?'

I nodded and nudged Leo. 'Got that?' I said. I gave his hand another squeeze, just to make amends.

'By the way, Maeve' continued Jamie, 'what were you blabbing about my grandad? Before ... before all this, you were going on about my grandad. Something about his nicking stuff. What was that about?'

I swallowed. Get out of this one, Maeve Morris.

'I, er,' I cleared my throat.

'Yes?'

'Well, I was putting two and two together and I thought that, maybe, your grandad – well you said yourself he needed money, so I thought ...'

'You thought my grandad was in on this?' His voice was angry, in spite of his own insistence on calm.

I nodded on miserably. 'Sorry,' I muttered. 'Should have known. But the way that Reilly used to look at us and scowl. And he's your grandad's right-hand man. I thought maybe they were both in on this.'

'You moron!' said Jamie. 'Grandad would be the last

one to be involved in something like this. Anyway, he's not hard up; by today's standards, he's pretty well heeled.'

'But you said ...'

'I said that it was hard to maintain the old house, but that wasn't to say that he's poverty stricken. You really are a twit to think that. And as for Reilly, it wasn't us he was scowling at. It was Fergus. He's been saying all along to grandad that Fergus is a bit dodgy, but grandad wouldn't listen to him. Now, look at how right he was.'

'He conned all of us,' I said, neatly shifting the conversation away from myself and my major gaff. 'We really thought he was a friend.'

'He used us to cement his relationship with grandad,' went on Jamie. 'All that horse-riding and teaching us to drive – it was just to wangle his way into grandad's good books. It was an innocent cover to keep him near the abbey so that he could oversee all of the stashing away of stolen artefacts. God, it makes me furious to think of it.'

'The creep,' I said with meaning. Thank goodness I hadn't declared my undying love to him. At least I was only an eejit inside my own head.

'I'd like to shove him in a sewer!' spat Leo.

'That's the spirit,' I approved.

All we could see was the distorted sky through the corrugated perspex above our heads. That same sky was over normal people out there; people going about their everyday lives, doing ordinary things like shopping or weeding or boiling cabbage. Suddenly these drop-dead boring things seemed like the most wonderful activities. I had never felt so isolated and troubled in my whole life.

11

Captives

Jamie let out a great sigh. I could feel it because I was jammed between him and Leo. I turned my head to look at him. His nose had stopped bleeding, but the blood had dried on his face and on the front of his sweatshirt. There was a red mark on his chin which would turn into a shiny bruise later.

'Are you all right?' was all I could think of to say. Daft I know, but scintillating conversation is a bit hard to rustle up at times like this. He smiled ruefully, glanced down at his bloody front and torn jeans and nodded.

'I'll survive,' he said.

Leo had begun struggling again. He was sobbing and grunting and, above all, dragging me into his struggles. I gritted my teeth. A panicky bug in me wanted to do that too – to keep struggling. But a couple of deep breaths restored common sense.

'Leave it, Leo,' I said. 'There's no point. You'll only get hot and upset.'

'I *am* hot and upset,' he muttered.

'She's right, Leo,' Jamie joined in. 'There's no point.'

Leo gave a few more squirms and tugs and, with a hiss of exasperation, went limp.

We sat in miserable silence for a few moments. The adrenalin that had come to our aid in the battle was now spent and the cold realisation that we were stuck here until God knows when was slowly creeping into our minds.

'We have to stay calm.' Jamie drove his point home again. 'Just remember, they can't keep us here forever.'

Another silence. Then a shout from Jamie, 'I've just thought of something.'

'What? What have you thought of?' I asked hopefully. Was he about to come up with some Great Plan?

'I left a note for grandad. Before I left this morning I left a note to say that I'd probably be over at your place, or else at the abbey. He'll find it when he gets back from the race-meeting.'

'So? What good will that do us?' asked Leo.

'Well, when I don't turn up for tea, grandad is sure to ring your folks ...'

'And discover that we're missing too,' I put in. 'And, since he's so afraid of kidnapping, like you said ...'

'He'll be on to the gardai straight away,' finished Jamie. 'Knowing grandad, there'll be a big search.'

'I don't see what good that will do,' Leo grumbled. Nor could I, for that matter, but Jamie seemed pleased with himself.

'It's a trump card,' he went on. 'The thoughts of strong gardai activity in the area might just scare them into letting us go ... even if it does mean letting us off miles away from here to give them a chance to get away. They'll have no choice but to lose us straight away. They'd never risk holding us here if they think the fuzz will be around. Now do you see?'

I nodded. 'Sounds good to me.' My heart began to thump as Jamie's words sank in. Hope!

'Yes,' said Leo, going all jittery again, this time with excitement. 'That's really cool, Jamie. It doesn't matter if they *do* take us miles away. We'll be free.'

'Right,' said Jamie. 'In the meantime we must stay very calm. Just bear in mind that we have the upper hand now.'

Jamie's optimism made us all a bit more cheerful. I could almost feel the wind through my hair after being let off in some remote mountainy place – I didn't care where, just so long as we were free. Bless Jamie, I thought, for being such a well brought up and thoughtful lad to leave a note for his grandad. There and then I resolved that, in the future, I too would be a well brought up young woman – even if I had to do it myself.

'You've got guts,' I said. 'Both of you.' I twisted around to include Leo in my praise. 'You both showed that crowd of ... of scumbags what you're made of.'

'You did OK yourself,' Jamie nudged me. He grinned. 'Celtic art has left its mark on Fergus.'

'Too right,' I said. 'Leo, please stop wriggling. Think about ... think about Indiana Jones or somebody.'

Leo sniffed and tried to wipe his nose on his shoulder. 'Get real, Maeve,' he muttered. But still he kept a hold of my hand. 'How long more do you think they'll be?' He raised his voice to include Jamie. Jamie shrugged, which meant that we all shrugged. They could at least have tied us individually instead of tying us together, the miserable creeps.

'Shouldn't be long,' said Jamie.

'What is it?' I asked. 'Their game I mean. What's the crooked deal?'

Jamie shrugged again. 'I wish you wouldn't do that,' I said. 'It drags me and Leo when you do it.'

'Sorry. What were you saying?'

'I asked what was their game.'

'It must be what my ... what Jim was talking about the other day,' said Leo. 'There's some kind of an international ring who buy up stuff like that for lots of money.'

I shook my head. 'I still can't understand what anyone would want with that junk.'

'I've told you, it's not junk, Maeve,' said Jamie. 'They're important things – artefacts – from the past. They can't be replaced so they're extremely rare. Collectors pay a bomb for things like that. These creeps are selling off part of Irish history to line their pockets. It's like ... it's like the country is being stripped bare of its heritage – *our* heritage.' He moved slightly to ease his cramped position. 'Soon there'll be nothing left in historic sites for people in the future to see. It will all have to be brought into museums for safety – what's left of it.'

'Cripes, I hadn't thought of it like that,' I said. Here was something else to be angry about. Leo wriggled a bit, but I hadn't the heart to tell him to stop again. He was scared and twitchy.

'What time is it?' he asked.

I twisted around so that I could see Jamie's watch.

'Ten to six.'

Leo sighed and looked thoughtful. 'Do you think they'll come back soon? Before that? The dark, I mean.' There was a catch in his voice.

'Bloody Fergus,' I said after a while.

'Too right, bloody Fergus,' agreed Jamie. 'Who'd have thought he'd be mixed up in a sleazy game like this? My grandad had great plans for him. Said he was the most efficient fellow he'd taken on for years.'

'He's efficient all right,' I muttered. 'He seems to be the big brain behind this scam. You need to be efficient to arrange scams.'

'I need to go to the loo,' Leo whimpered.

So did I, but I remembered that Jamie had called me a lady and ladies do not declare that they're bursting to go to the loo. I stole a glance at Jamie. I hadn't noticed before how his chin jutted, giving his lower lip a decisive assertiveness. His nose was slightly squashed in the middle, as if it has been broken some time in the past (if it had been broken in the recent fight it would be all red and swollen). This gave him an aura of mystery and made his face stop short of being too handsome. I wanted to reach out and wash the dried blood from his upper lip. As if he sensed my eyes on him, he turned to look at me.

'Does ... does your face hurt?' I covered my tracks with an inane question.

'No. It probably looks worse than it is. What about you? Fergus gave you a right thump.'

'It's OK. I probably won't be able to wear my strapless evening gown for a while, but that's not important.'

Jamie nodded and smiled. 'You're ... you're pretty cool, Maeve,' he said. 'Different.'

That was the nicest think anyone had ever said to me in my whole life. For a moment I forgot that we were tied up in a grotty shed, waiting for a load of gangsters to come back and decide our fate.

We slipped into silence. Nobody seemed to have anything to say. Words brought no consolation. Now and then one of us would move to try and ease cramped limbs.

The beautiful Miss Morris swept the candle from her

bedside and wandered around the room, pressing knobs on the fireplace and tapping the wainscotting. Old houses like this always had secret chambers and things from the days when people needed to hide from enemies who always seemed to be lurking about then. She glanced out of the window. The line of evil-doers had passed beyond the estate walls and were out on the moor, their ghostly glow like a luminous dragon stretched out along the dark landscape. She resumed her frantic search.

'Bingo ... I mean Gadzooks!' she cried as a hollow sound met her gentle tapping. She felt about behind a picture of a hairy cow standing in mucky water and found a lever. When she pulled it, nothing happened for a moment and her heart sank. Then, ever so slowly, a small bookcase began to turn on an axis. A chill, damp breeze emanated from the opening and Miss Morris gagged. What was in this scary passage?

With brave decisiveness, she forced herself to take an extra candle and venture forth. Spiral steps led downwards. They seemed to go on forever. Down, down, deeper and deeper she went, her heart fluttering with fear of what might lie ahead, but her anger forcing her to go on.

Eventually the walls changed in texture from brick to solid stone. Even the smell had changed from old mustiness to a sharper, salty one. She was in a cave. The candle spluttered and began to get dim. Miss Morris was glad she'd brought an extra one which she slotted into the holder. Her limbs ached and she felt that if this passage didn't open out soon, she would just lie down and die. Then, as she rounded a bend in the narrow cave, she saw a pale blue light ahead and heard the distant sound of water. The cave opened out into a large chamber.

She held aloft the candle and gasped in dismay at the array

*of goods stacked around the walls; boxes and boxes with
'GOLD BULLION' stamped on their sides, rolls of Chinese silk,
crates of wine, bags of glittering jewellery, chests with highly
polished silver chalices in them and valuable statues wrapped
in sacking that made them look like corpses. As she moved
about, the glow from the candle threw big, distorted shadows
on to the cavern walls. 'This is where they store their ill-gotten
stuff,' thought the beautiful Miss Morris. 'This is the cave I
saw them moving stuff into this morning.' No wonder Pickaxe
had materialised so swiftly; she'd used the secret passage to get
back to the pink room and up to the attic where Lord
Chiselchin and she had been.*

*And now, tonight, there would be an extra load to add to the
treasure. And another cargo of dead sailors would sink into the
depths of the cruel sea, to have their bones picked white by the
creatures that lurked there. 'I must warn them,' she thought. 'I
simply must warn them or die in the attempt. These gorillas …
these wicked people must not get away with this.'*

*She ran to the cave mouth and began the steep climb up the
face of the rocky cliff. Her beautifully manicured nails were
torn and bleeding, but she struggled on. 'I must make it,' she
gasped. The wind whipped the tiny shoe from her dainty foot
and cast it into the water below.*

I looked down at my feet in the dim light. 'Oh no,' I
groaned.

'What is it?' Jamie stirred.

'My Docs.'

'Your what?'

'My good Doc Martens. There's a dirty great tear on
one of them.'

'Is that all? I thought you were bleeding to death.'

'I saved for these sixteen-hole Docs for months. Now I'm really angry. I'll kill those filthy creeps when they come back. So help me I will.'

'You might get your chance now,' whispered Jamie. 'Listen.'

We held our breath and listened to the sound of a car driving over gravel. There was a squeak as it pulled up close by. We waited for the sound of the shed doors opening, but all went quiet again.

'Do you think they've forgotten we're here?' Leo asked nervously. By now we must have been here several hours and the discomfort was mega. We were holding out really well, I thought, after Jamie's pep-talk. Leo's hand was pretty sweaty (well, could have been mine, I suppose; but ladies are not as sweaty as blokes so it was probably Leo). Still, I kept a comforting hold on him.

'No such luck, dear cousin,' I tried to laugh. 'They'll be in to do their little war-dance around us, you wait and see.'

Sure enough, dead on cue, the doors swung open and feet rustled through the loose hay on the shed floor.

'What the hell kept you?' I recognised Fergus's voice.

'I've a business to run, haven't I?' a whine with a vaguely familiar tone to it replied. Where had I heard it before? I'm very good at recognising voices. It comes of hanging about under the staff-room window with my pal, Siobhan, to hear if any of the teachers were talking about us. This particular voice didn't belong to any of the abbey group. But it just wouldn't come to me. I hadn't time to figure it out now anyway.

'Yeah, sure. While we do all the donkey work.' Fergus again.

'Put a sock in it, Fergus. If it wasn't for my legit business you lot would be like a boat without a tiller.'

A boat? Boat. Why did that jog my memory? Boat. Yacht. Yacht! Of course. The button with the yacht on it! The one I'd found in the abbey and the one that had been under the chalice. *Now* I remembered: O'Rourke, the auctioneer. That was why I'd a hazy association of him being somehow untidy that day he'd called to Aunt Brid; there had been buttons missing from his blazer which stood out in stark contrast to the rest of his squeaky clean appearance. The remaining buttons were just like the ones I'd found. So, O'Rourke was in on this too. The skunk. And him trying to wheedle Aunt Brid and Jim from their cottage.

The bales were pulled back and a torch shone into our eyes. We recoiled from the dazzling light. It was unnerving to hear the voices without being able to see the faces.

'Are you going to let us out?' Leo was struggling, which made the twine dig into my arms.

'At least you could untie us,' Jamie's voice was more reasonable. 'We're hardly going to do a runner ...'

'Tell me about it,' sneered Dave.

'Yes, I will tell you about it,' said Jamie with the amazing calm that could only come from holding a trump card. Let them have it, Jamie, I thought. He leaned towards the voices, which meant of course that we all did. 'I've left a note for my grandad,' he continued evenly. 'I told him where I was going. When he finds I'm not there he'll have every garda in town out looking for me. Have no doubt about it,' he added with relished emphasis. 'This place will be crawling with police before you know it ...'

'So you'd better let us free,' interrupted Leo. 'You can take us to the mountains or … or anywhere and get away yourselves. Just let us go. Before the gardai come. Now.'

I breathed a sigh, wishing I could see their faces after that bombshell. They'd be angry, but they'd have no option but to let us go.

'A note you say?' the voice belonged to Fergus.

'Yes,' Jamie almost spat the word. 'And you know my grandad, he'll have every …'

'So you said,' put in Fergus. There was a rustling sound, then he thrust a piece of paper into the torchlight. 'Would this be the note?' he asked.

I could feel Jamie stiffen. 'How did you …' he began.

Fergus gave a nasty laugh. 'Found it in his study, didn't I? Didn't want him nosing about the abbey so I ... er ... borrowed your note.'

There was more laughter now from the rest of the thugs. I felt like I'd been hit by a train. All our hopes had been focused on that little bit of paper and now there was nothing left to cling to.

Jamie kicked out in frustration. 'You're a maggot, Fergus,' he growled. 'A slimy maggot. And you'd no business in my grandad's study.'

Fergus laughed again.

'Jeez!' O'Rourke spoke now, keeping his voice to a low whisper, obviously playing safe. 'So these are the snoops. Good job you caught them on time. Are you sure no one saw you?'

'I'm not a fool,' snapped Fergus.

'OK, OK. Keep your hair on. Put the hay back and keep those little brats out of my sight.'

The thoughts of being entombed again filled me with bladder-bursting panic. 'I need to go to the bathroom,' I shouted. 'You've got to let us out of here.'

'Damn!' someone swore on the other side of the hay wall.

They lowered their voices and we strained to hear what was being said.

'What's your suggestion?' I think it was Dave's voice.

There was a pause. 'Rotten bloody luck.' O'Rourke again. 'At least the consignment is just complete and ready to go. Things could be worse, a whole lot worse. All we have to do is keep these brats out of the way until the stuff is on its way. By then you lot will be gone and so will all trace of the stuff.'

'Recognise them, those kids?' That was Fergus.

O'Rourke's answer was lost as he lowered his voice to a whisper again. All we could hear after that was a low buzz. I was getting mad by now; I'd had quite enough of this cruddy game, thank you very much. My legs and arms were numb and I was in pain. And that business about the note made me want to scream. Anger! Stay angry, Maeve. I took a sharp breath.

'Let us out of here!' I shouted. 'We need a loo, and food. You can't treat us like ...'

'Shut up.' A gruff voice which I didn't recognise.

'I won't shut up.' Now was the time to play *my* trump card. 'I know it's you out there, O'Rourke, Mister Respectable Auctioneer. I know you're up to your hairy armpits in this and you'll be sorry. You'll be holding your next auction in Mountjoy jail.' There, let him mull over that little lot. And my voice didn't shake even once.

A really rude word broke the momentary silence. Ha! That had got them going.

There was another rude word to echo that, but this time it was beside me. Jamie snorted with disgust. What was eating him? I'd put the wind up that lot out there and he was swearing.

'Maeve!' he hissed, 'you shouldn't have said that. Now we're in deeper than ever. If they know we can positively identify O'Rourke, they've no option but to ... to, God, I don't know what they'll do now.'

12

Shady Deals

Leo gave a whimper and struggled some more. I bit my lip. I was so sure I'd done the right thing, putting that sleazebag O'Rourke in his place. Seemed now that I was wrong. I hate being wrong, it upsets me deeply, sours my outlook on life. So I did the only thing that any self-respecting feminist can do when the odds are stacked against her, I opened my mouth very wide and began to bawl at the top of my voice. A superbly orchestrated, full-bodied, hair-curling outburst that did proud to my gender. Mrs Pankhurst, sod the vote; when the chips are down the only answer is good, old-fashioned hysterics. That brought them running, I can tell you.

'Shut up!' shouted a voice as anxious hands tore away the bales. We were practically lifted across to the house and the twine cut away before you could say 'suckers!'

I caught a glimpse of O'Rourke's puce face before I was ushered to a downstairs loo by Mossy. The two boys were pushed upstairs. Bandy-legged Mossy stood guard outside while I went in and locked the door. It was a small, smelly loo with no seat and a filthy handbasin. There was only a tiny, dusty window with a lacework of cobwebs around it. The glass was broken and wire mesh had been used to patch up the whole window on the outside.

Though I was simply dying to go, I suddenly dried up at the thoughts of Mossy outside, within hearing distance. Then I hit on the bright idea of flushing the loo while I peed. Then of course I had to wait until the cistern filled up again so that I could make a genuine flush.

'What the hell are you at in there?' Mossy growled.

'Mind your own business,' I said, examining the ceiling to see if there might be a panel one could climb through. No such luck. However, I stood on the WC and picked a bit of glass from the window. It might prove useful.

'Come on!' growled Mossy.

I smirked. I'd milk this little bit of freedom for all it was worth. Just for kicks, I flushed the loo again and washed my Docs.

Back in the kitchen there was wall-to-wall tension as the white-faced men stood ill at ease and wondered what to do with us. I felt this great need to see my fourteenth birthday and worked my mind back into angry determination.

'Sit there.' Fergus pointed to where Leo and Jamie were sitting at a table in the corner. 'Try anything funny and I won't be responsible for the consequences,' he added.

I squeezed in beside Leo. Jamie nodded to me. He was rubbing his arms and wrists.

'Neat scars,' I said, rolling up my own sleeves. A network of red weals criss-crossed the whole length of each arm. 'I hope they last a good while. They'll make for groovy conversation.'

Jamie give me one of those 'you can't be for real' looks, smiled and shook his head. He had made some attempt at wiping the blood from his lip, but Leo was as grimy as ever. Poor Leo. All that self-inflicted tension at home; some sort of pathetic guilt over his dead father driving him to convince himself that Jim didn't love him and, most probably, that he shouldn't love Jim. And now this. He must be feeling totally screwed up, I thought. I put my arm around him and he looked up at me with his tear-stained face.

'Back off,' he grunted.

Mossy put three mugs of tea in front of us, and a plate of bread slathered with what my father calls make-believe butter. We looked at one another and wondered if we should take a stand against our jailers by refusing the food; a sort of hunger-strike to make them worry. But the thought passed very fleetingly and we fell on the bread and tea. The men continued to talk in low, anxious tones at the other end of the kitchen. It was a dismal place, all vinyl and tubular steel. There were socks drying on a shelf over the range and the whole room smacked of neglect.

'Is this O'Rourke's hovel?' I asked Leo.

He nodded. 'Think so,' he said. 'I know he lives a bit out of town and this is a bit out of town. The other fellas are not local.'

I ran my hand over the greasy table-top. 'Yecchh. Has his missus never trained him to use a bit of Jif?'

'He's not married,' said Leo. 'He's a bachelor.'

I sniffed and looked around. 'That figures,' I said. 'His father was probably a bachelor too.' Jamie snorted a laugh and Leo looked puzzled.

Now that we were away from that smelly shed and had been fed, we were feeling a little more human. It's amazing how people adapt to the most awful situations – like those women in 'Tenko', a television programme I used to watch with my mother about these women who were in a Japanese prison-camp. They never let their spirits get submerged. I always felt I'd be just as good. I never thought, of course, that I'd have to prove it.

'I bet they're wondering.' Leo cut across my thoughts.

'Who?'

'At home. I bet they're worried, Ma and Jamie's grandad.'

'And Jim,' I added crisply.

Jamie shook his head and looked up from the crumbs of bread he was gathering into a damp, grey ball between his finger and thumb. 'Not yet,' he said. 'They'll only be at the angry stage now – thinking we're gone on a hike or something. The worry bit will come later.'

We jumped as the telephone rang. O'Rourke grabbed it and the others watched his face as he listened. He seemed to look relieved and was nodding. Every now and then he said 'Yes,' or 'OK,' or 'Righto'. It was a short conversation. When he put down the phone, he bared his heavy-duty dentures to the others in an attempted grin.

'It's all systems go, lads,' he said. 'The stuff has been loaded into a truck disguised as a Board of Works vehicle and is on its way here.'

'All of it?' asked Dave in amazement.

'All of it.' O'Rourke rubbed his hands.

'That was quick work,' said Fergus.

'Patsy and his crew work fast,' said O'Rourke. 'As soon as I got your message, I was on the car-phone to Patsy. He got things moving straight away. He had to, didn't he? Too much resting on this lot for all of us.'

'What about ... ?' Mossy nodded in our direction. Heads turned to look at us. O'Rourke stood up. Nobody spoke as he swayed back and forth, deep in thought.

'We'll say nothing.' Was I really saying this? The words just seemed to slip out in quiet desperation. 'We'll wait until you've gone and we'll say nothing.'

'Yeah, sure,' said Dave. 'You love us that much.'

O'Rourke had stopped swaying. 'I'll deal with the kids,' he said. 'You lot head for the ferry later, as planned. I'll deal with these. Get them out of the way for now, until we've got the carrier packed.'

Fergus cast a slightly anxious glance in our direction. 'How do you mean to deal with them?' he asked in a low voice.

O'Rourke frowned. 'Never you mind about that. You just concentrate on getting on to that ferry. Got your passports, everybody?'

Fergus hesitated. My heart leapt. Was he feeling ever so slightly concerned about us? Was our friendship worth something after all? He seemed to be about to say something, but it passed.

O'Rourke turned to Mossy and Dave. 'Put them in the box-room upstairs.' He pointed at us and my heart sank. The ordeal wasn't over yet.

Suddenly everyone was busy. 'Let's get moving,' Dave urged, grabbing Leo's arm.

'It's all right. We're coming,' I snapped. 'We don't have to be dragged.'

Mossy went ahead of us up the stairs and Dave guarded the rear. The stair carpet was worn and dusty. Brown wood panels came halfway up the stair wall. The rest was covered with slime green paint through which some cracks appeared. I got the impression that O'Rourke had simply been using the house as a stopping-off point over the past few years while he was amassing the antiquities in the abbey. He'd probably sell out now and live on his fortune in luxury somewhere – probably out of the country.

Mossy had opened a door off the landing. 'In here, and don't try anything. There are people coming who won't be messed about, so keep your traps shut and make like you're not here.'

'Are you going to tie us up?' Leo asked, with a hint of fear in his voice.

Mossy looked back at Dave who shook his head. 'I don't think you'll get out of this room, sonny. Window's too small and the door's got a massive lock – O'Rourke is very security conscious,' he added with a laugh.

The window was indeed very small and quite high up. Light, which was filtering in from what I thought must be the yard, was just strong enough for us to see our new nick. A mattress on the floor had stuffing and springs protruding from it, giving it the appearance of some sort of flabby extra-terrestrial with curly antennae. Trashy furniture lay scattered about, some of it overturned. Leo set one of the chairs straight and tried to look out of the window, but he was way too short. Between us we righted a table and stood the chair on top of that.

'I'll have a look,' Jamie said to Leo. 'With my height I'll just about make it.'

We held the table as he clambered up.

'Well?' I asked.

'Hold on,' said Jamie, wiping the dirt off the tiny window. 'We're overlooking the yard.'

'What's happening?'

'Nothing yet. Wait now, a couple of blokes have gone over to a big shed.'

'Is it the one we were in?' asked Leo.

'No. It's much bigger. They're opening the doors.'

'Yes?'

'Nothing. The doors are just open, that's it. Oh, there are lights moving into the yard.'

'What sort of lights?' I wished I was up there. I hate finding out things second-hand.

'Headlights. Wow! It's a huge truck. One of those big international things.'

'Get down and let me see,' Impatience got the better of me.

'There's really nothing more to see.' Jamie looked down at me. 'It's only a big truck. There's nothing else happening yet.'

'I'd still like to see. You've been up there a good while now.'

'Oh, all right.' He jumped down and held the table while I got up. Sure enough, a great big truck had backed up to the open door of the shed. There was no sign of anyone around and I was about to get down when there were more lights. Another, smaller truck pulled up beside the first one. Suddenly there was action everywhere as men sprang into action.

'You've got to see this,' I said to the other two, without intending to give up my position. 'Get another chair and we'll balance it beside this one.'

They did, and then the two boys climbed up beside me. Leo put his two elbows on the ledge and Jamie and I held him there. There was just enough room for the three of us to see out.

A forklift truck appeared from the large shed with what appeared to be sack loaded on the front.

'Fertiliser,' declared Leo. 'They're bags of fertiliser.'

'Fertiliser?' I exclaimed. 'Are you sure?'

Leo nearly lost his balance as he turned to give me a scathing look.

'I'd know those bags anywhere,' he said. 'Ma uses that fertiliser all the time. O'Rourke's Healthigro it's called.'

'O'Rourke?' said Jamie. 'That must be his front, as well as the auctioneering business.'

'What do you mean by that?' I had hoped that Leo would ask the question. I don't like showing my ignorance.

'It means that he has an ordinary, respectable business as a cover for his shady deals. What could be more innocent for an auctioneer-cum-fertiliser manufacturer than to have big trucks coming and going? Who'd suspect anything?'

'Surely he must be making enough money with his ordinary business without having to pinch old stuff – heritage stuff,' I said. This was still quite beyond me.

'Greed,' said Jamie. 'The dollar is god to people like him.'

'Wouldn't the people in the bank know that he had more money than he should?' I persisted. 'Surely someone would spot that. Income tax people. My dad says they're born fully grown with special radar that can detect an extra pound coin in someone's pocket at a distance of two miles.'

Jamie laughed and disturbed a cobweb from which a spider had long departed. 'This is international business,' he explained. 'He probably has a safe bank account in Switzerland.'

'Coo,' I said. 'There's that much money in old stuff?'

'He probably deals in other things as well.'

'Look,' Leo's voice interrupted. 'They're taking something out of the other truck.'

We strained to see better and nearly knocked the two chairs. As Leo said, some of the men were unloading heavy things from the smaller truck and carrying them on to the big one. Then the forklift would drive up the ramp with a load of fertiliser bags.

Jamie whistled. 'See. They're putting the stolen stuff between the bags of fertiliser. Who would ever suspect anything? Clever.'

'And the sacks of fertilizer would act like cushions so that nothing gets broken,' I added.

'Makes you sick, doesn't it?' said Jamie as we got down from our perch. There was no point in hanging on up there now. We knew what was going on. 'To think that that lot are getting away with this and there's nothing we can do about it.'

That served to remind us that there was still the question of what was to be done with us. The prospect filled me with that awful chill which, this time, wouldn't go away.

13

Can Things Get Any Worse?

'Well at least this place is better than being tied up in that stinking shed,' I said. 'I wonder why they didn't lock us up here from the beginning.'

'I'd say it was because they intended keeping O'Rourke's identity a secret from us. Probably would have blindfolded us when they'd move us. But since you ... since they realised we knew who he was, there was little point in keeping us out there.'

'That's daft,' said Leo. 'Sure we saw the place when we came here with Fergus. We'd be able to tell the gardai ...'

Jamie was shaking his head. 'By then everything would be moved, every shred of evidence. Who do you think the cops would believe, a respectable pillar of town and church or three upstarts like us?'

'But the abbey ...' I began. 'We could have shown them the abbey.'

Jamie shook his head again. 'Do you honestly think they'd leave that secret chamber? They'd make sure to fix it so that nobody would get in again – ever.'

I looked at Jamie with open-mouthed awe for a couple of seconds. He had an answer for everything. I was glad he was with us – I felt we could depend on him. He had that quiet confidence that makes you feel everything will be OK. Even if the note thing had been a disaster, I still felt more comfortable having him here.

He sank on to the mattress and rested his elbows on his knees. There was a tense frown on his brow which put a slight wobble on my faith in him. Leo sat down beside him. 'What are you thinking, Jamie?' he asked.

Jamie let out a sharp sigh and rubbed the bruise on his chin.

'I'm thinking about O'Rourke,' he said.

'I can think of better things,' I said. 'Like rotten fish or diarrhoea ...'

'He's dangerous,' Jamie went on. 'He knows we can identify him. It's different with those others – they'll disappear. But O'Rourke, well he's from the town. Like I said, he's established here – has a reputation. A respectable reputation?'

'What are you getting at, Jamie?' The cold chill seemed to grip my neck even tighter.

'What I'm saying ...' Jamie seemed to be having difficulty getting the right words. 'What I'm saying is that he can't let us go. At least not unless he decides to up and leave with the others on the ferry. And ...'

'Go on,' prompted Leo.

'And he can't do that. He can't suddenly leave behind a thriving business and ... and this house and his estate agency. He wouldn't just throw all that away just because of ... of us.'

'You mean he's going to keep us locked up here?' a note of hysteria was creeping into Leo's voice. 'Is that what you mean, Jamie?'

'No,' Jamie muttered. He seemed sorry he'd started this conversation.

'What then?'

'Oh my God!' I burst out. 'Do you think he's going to kill us?'

'Oh no!' Leo began to howl. 'Oh no, Jamie. Don't say

that. Please don't say that.' He bawled. I sat beside him and rocked him in my arms. This time he didn't push me away.

'Now see what you've done,' I hissed at Jamie over Leo's head. 'You've scared the bejapers out of the child.'

'It's your doing,' Jamie snarled back at me and my world fell apart. 'If you hadn't opened your big mouth and said you knew O'Rourke we'd have been let off later. Now there's no way we're going to get out of here ...'

Alive! I knew his next word would be 'alive', but he glanced at the sobbing Leo and didn't say it.

'That's right, blame me,' I spat. 'Whose idea was it to show us that stupid manuscript in the first place? And who suggested that we look for the stupid hole in the ground?'

'And who went to see what was going on last night at the abbey?' he retorted. 'And,' his eye gleamed with triumph, 'whose monumentally crazy idea was it to run to Fergus with our find? I wanted to go straight to the gardai. If we'd done that, these creeps would be behind bars now and we'd be at home – safe. The ball is firmly in your court, Maeve. You're the one who got us into this.'

'You're ... I hate you!' I was sobbing myself at this stage. 'I wish we'd never met you.'

'Yeah. Well, ditto with me.' Jamie sank his head into his hands. 'You're ... you're like something from a bad American film,' he continued. 'Your use of English is on a level with those obnoxious Beavis and Butthead dopes.'

'You're a poncy Brit!' I was shaking. 'Drop dead.' Bad choice of words, but they slipped out.

Leo raised his head. 'Maeve, I'm scared.' He had

stopped crying. Now he was hiccuping.

I glared at Jamie and he glared back. I rocked back and forth with Leo and tried to calm him. Jamie, my last prop in this whole mess, had left me floundering and guilty. I felt I was falling into a black hole of despair.

We all sank into a terrified silence. We could hear the voices down below. So long as we could hear them, I thought, we were all right. It was when the men and the trucks would leave that we should worry. I clutched Leo's bony shoulders and tried to force my mind away from the D word.

The beautiful Miss Morris continued to climb up the slippery cliff, her bare foot torn from the rough surface. At last she reached the top. She stood and looked about her, trying to find a landmark that would tell her where she was.

She heaved a sigh of relief as she saw, in the distance, the twinkling lights of Goodleigh Cove, the harbour where the Spanish ship was really supposed to dock. She tore off her linen petticoat and wrapped it around her foot. Then she set off across the dark moor. Would she be on time to save the sailors?

Many times she tripped over unseen roots and tree stumps, but not once did she waver in her determination to see this thing through. Mercifully the lights were becoming ever closer. Soon, soon, she told herself, I'll be there soon. Just then she tripped once more, but this time she was unable to get up. She was sinking in a slimy bog-hole that was pulling her into its mushy centre.

'Help!' she cried out. But who was to hear her in this isolated place? She could feel the fingers of death close around her.

Leo had calmed down a bit, his head resting on my chest. His sobbing had stopped and he seemed to have been lulled into the sort of peace that comes when you're so sobbed out that you haven't the energy to raise another snivel. I've been there so I knew the form (except that this crying wasn't carefully staged to get permission to go to a disco for fifteen year-olds or a protest at being made to take piano-lessons instead of getting an electric guitar).

'Maeve.' I nearly leapt out of my skin when Jamie touched my arm.

'What do you want?' My voice was a squeak.

'I'm sorry. We're scared and tense. It got out of hand. I'm sorry. Forget what I said. It was a load of cobblers. I didn't mean any of it.'

'Yeah, well.' I tried to take this in. No one had ever apologised to me before – especially when what they'd said was true. There was no doubt but my mother was right when she said that good breeding shows. The sort of boys I knew would have sulked forever or else shouted me down. Here was a man of thirteen going on fifty-five. Well, I could rise to the occasion too. In carefully chosen words I said, 'I apologise too. Let's simply forget the whole episode.'

There was silence again. I had nothing more to say, but at least it was a slightly more comfortable silence. It had got cold and I looked around in the hope that there might be an old blanket or something. No such luck. I shivered and Leo stretched himself as if from a sleep. We had to do something to keep ourselves from turning into head cases. What do you do, locked in a small room knowing that the dice is loaded against you? I remembered my father telling me about Brian Keenan, a man who was kept locked up in a small space in Beirut with a couple of other prisoners for about four years, not knowing if they were going to live or die. They'd kept their spirits alive by silly games and jokes. Worth a try. There were no madmen with tea-towels on their heads outside, but there certainly was a bunch of thugs.

'Let's play I Spy,' I said.

Leo shook his head.

'Yes, we will,' I insisted. 'Come on. I spy something beginning with …' (there was hardly enough stuff to cover even a fraction of the alphabet, but at least it would stop Leo descending into a feverish terror) '… B,' I finished. 'I spy something beginning with B. Come on, Leo. You're always asking me to play this with you. What begins with B?'

Leo gave a desultory glance around. 'Dunno,' he muttered. This was going to be hard work.

'Bum,' put in Jamie. 'Is it bum?'

A trace of a smile crossed Leo's face.

'Nope,' I replied, looking at Leo for his guess.

'Bananas,' Jamie piped in.

'There are no bananas.' Leo was hooked. I looked gratefully at Jamie. He was all right, this poncy Brit.

So we kept our spirits alive with silly word-games and rude jokes. It was only when we heard engines starting up that we were jolted back to awful reality.

We sat in silence and waited.

14

The Bog

We instinctively bunched together when we heard footsteps coming up the stairs. Each step added forty years to my life so that, by the time they stopped, I felt like I'd gone way past my sell-by date and was just a quivering, geriatric blob.

'Don't make any sudden moves,' a muffled voice called from outside. There was the jangle of a key in the lock and the door swung open. Against the light of the landing were silhouetted O'Rourke and Mossy, who I recognised by the curved light between his bandy legs. O'Rourke turned on the light, a weak naked bulb that simply made worse the dreariness of the room.

They were both carrying baseball bats. Was this it? Were we about to be clubbed to death with the tools of an American game? If I hadn't been to the bathroom earlier, I'd have wet my knickers I was that scared. Most of me wanted to curl up and whimper, plead, grovel, snivel and say 'Please mister, don't harm us'. But one small, insistent beat tried to get its message through the cloud of panic and into my dysfunctioning brain. 'Be angry,' it said. Anger! That was the only weapon in this nightmare. I gritted my teeth. I needed something to focus on so that I could get angry. I looked at Leo, his small, bony body shrunk even more with fear as he cowered between me and Jamie. His face was filthy except for the clean tracks from tears. One cheek was red under the grime where he'd been clobbered earlier. His

hair stuck up like a bad mix of grunge and punk. The weals on his arms from the baler twine seemed more pathetic with the goose-bumps between. The poor kid must have been frozen; his sweater had disappeared ages ago, along with the chalice.

But it was his tee-shirt that kick-started my anger. It had a picture of a smiling dolphin on the front, with 'Save the Dolphin' written in a circle around it. That was my cousin Leo all right; save the dolphin, save the rain forests, save the world, save ants, bats, frogs, butterflies, ladybirds. How many times had I poked through his bookshelves for something to read and jeered at his collection of well-thumbed books on nature and stuff? He was just a harmless little boy and nobody had any right to fill him with this terror. I gripped him and put him behind me. I had every intention of putting up the most vicious fight – Maeve Morris would not go down like a trapped rat – more like a supersonic shrew.

'Just do as you're told now and everything will be all right,' O'Rourke was saying. 'Nobody will get hurt. Sure we only want to keep you for a little while longer and then you'll be able to go home. This will all be over shortly.' His voice was wheedling and set off warning bells in my head. People who wheedle either have done, or are about to do, something rotten. The wheedle veils the guilt. I know; I could write a book on The Wheedle.

'Where are you taking us?' Jamie asked, his assertive chin thrust forward, like a beacon, with the red bruise coming up nicely.

Mossy was tapping himself on the knee with the baseball bat. You could see that he was only dying to hear the delightful thunk of it smashing into Jamie's body.

O'Rourke made a great show of being patient. 'Now look, sonny. It's your own meddling got you into this. Can't you see that we have to hold you until things are sorted out our end? You just stay quiet until then and everyone will be happy. You'll be off home, the three of you. You understand that, don't you?'

Jamie grimaced. 'Why not just leave us here?' he reasoned. 'Go away and get your ... your business deal done and then send someone back to free us? What's the point in moving us? It's secure here. We can't get out.'

'Nice try, Jamie,' I thought. 'But, for a brainbox like yourself, bloody pathetic.'

Mossy pointed the baseball bat at Jamie. 'Shut it, fella,' he said. 'And listen to the man. Do as you're told and everything will be fine. A hint of trouble and ...' he prodded Jamie in the chest. Jamie bristled. Oh no, not more heroics. I caught his arm and he backed down.

'Now there'll be no need for any of that.' O'Rourke was wheedling again. 'Easy on there now, Mossy. They're going to be real sensible kiddies and do what they're told. Aren't you, folks?'

The heavy-duty dentures bared again and I thought I'd throw up.

'Now, Mossy here is going to have to tie you up, you understand that, don't you? It will only be for a little while, but we can't risk losing you, heh, heh.'

You'd think he was organising party games, the old sleazebag. We'd no choice but to stand still while Mossy produced more baler twine and tied us together. I so wanted to kick him where it hurt, but I knew that would serve no useful purpose. I was nursing my precious anger until the bitter end. I glanced at Jamie and I could see that he felt the same. He caught my eye and shook his head slightly. Smashed skulls wouldn't help our case.

'Ouch, you're hurting me,' Leo shouted. He pulled away from Mossy.

'OK, son. Just stand easy and Mossy won't hurt you again, right, Mossy?'

Mossy scowled and continued to tie Leo's arms behind his back.

We were ushered downstairs, through the kitchen and into the empty yard. A Hiace van, with its doors open, stood just across from the back door. Mossy lifted Leo and pushed him in. He reached out to do the same for me, but I swung away from him and climbed in myself. I'd amputate any part of my body that he'd touch. Maeve – legless and armless but pure.

There was nothing in the back of the van; nothing that we could prop ourselves against except for a crude wall of chipboard with a perspex window that separated the driver's cabin from the back. We settled ourselves well away from there. We were bounced around as the van twisted and turned along the road. Leo stood unsteadily, peering ahead through the perspex to try and recognise landmarks.

'I think we're headed towards the bog,' he murmured as he knelt down and we leaned our heads together.

'Do you mean we're passing by your house?' I asked.

He shook his head. 'Different bog,' he said. 'Maher's bog. It's bigger and wilder.'

'Does it lead somewhere, this road?' I asked hopefully. 'Other than the bog?'

Jamie and I exchanged worried looks. Anyone who knew bogland well enough would know where to dispose of three thin bodies without fear of discovery. O'Rourke would know what parts were being used for turf cutting and what parts were wilderness.

The sudden change from road to rough track caused us to be tossed around like fleas in a tumble drier, thus preventing me from crying out in the panic that had finally overcome me. Bounce, bounce, shake, shake. It was agony. I looked helplessly at Leo, all my good anger gone. There was nothing left but real fear. Leo had a grin on his face and his eyes were open wide as he stared at me. Jeez, I thought. The child has gone into a pre-death fit. Hallucinating. He was probably seeing his ancestors, in white frocks, waiting at the mouth of a heavenly tunnel. I'd read about stuff like that. I swallowed hard. I had no particular wish to see dead ancestors – in Dazwhite frocks or otherwise, thank you very much.

'Leo ...' I began.

He held up his hands. My jaw fell open. Jamie acted quickly, slithering nearer to Leo and indicating to me to do the same.

'Don't wave your hands about,' he hissed, glancing at the heads behind the perspex window. 'Sit down.'

'It was all the shaking,' Leo began. 'And that creep didn't tie the knots tight after I shouted that time ...'

'Never mind that,' Jamie said abruptly. 'Just untie us.'

We were still being bounced about, but Leo managed to untangle the twine from our hands. When we were free I was all on for trying to kick the door open. But Jamie had other ideas.

'Pretend that we're still tied up,' he said. 'Then, here's what we'll do.'

We huddled together to hear what Jamie had to say against the noise and the shaking. Leo and I nodded when he'd finished. We wrapped the twine around our arms and sat still. The tension was awful.

The van backed slowly and we swayed at it did a U-turn, leaving it facing the way it had come. We'd stopped, but the engine was still running. For a quick getaway after shoving us into a bog-hole, I thought bitterly. The doors creaked open with heartstopping finality. A torch shone in on us.

'Out,' growled O'Rourke. No wheedling – no more Mr Nice Guy. I really knew now that his own survival was his prime concern. There was no way he was ever going to let us blow his cover. Not ever.

15

A Frantic Drive

Jamie eased himself out first, his hands pressed behind his back. I followed, then Leo. As Jamie had told us, we put up a very good show of being cowed and snivelling. Except for the torch held by Mossy, the ominous black of the sky merged with the bog. Far away the lights of the town reflected with a faint glow on to the light clouds. This was no time to admire the scenery.

'Now!' shouted Jamie, throwing away the twine and dashing to the left of the track. His action took the two men by surprise and they both instinctively made a dive after him. I was about to dash in the other direction when Leo caught my arm and half dragged me to the front of the van.

'What are you ...?' I spluttered as he opened the door on the driver's side. This was not part of the plan. He and I were supposed to go in the opposite direction to Jamie and split Mossy and O'Rourke. Now, what Jamie had really hoped for had happened – both men were chasing him. And now Leo was about to screw this up. There was no way I'd leave him and here he was, doing something stupid.

I glanced back and saw a light heading this way. They'd got their act together and one of them was coming back to see to us.

'Get in!' shouted Leo. He was already fumbling with the gears and the Hiace was starting to move. The torchlight was galloping nearer. I jumped into the moving van. I'd like to say that I looked frantically around for Jamie, but the only thing on my mind was self-preservation.

Whoever was carrying the torch was almost on us now. He was shouting incoherently.

'Leo ...' I slammed the door and locked it.

'It's all right. Hang on.' Leo's head was barely high enough to see out over the steering-wheel, and he had to perch on the edge of the seat to reach the pedals. I screamed as a face appeared at the window on my side. It was O'Rourke and he was not mouthing pleasantries. He was pulling at the handle with one hand and pounding at the window with the other. The torchlight flashed back and forth with each blow, giving his face a dramatically demonic appearance. The van shot forward and stopped, then forward again. Each time it lurched to a stop, the face appeared again. One more lurch. No face.

'We've shaken him off,' I shouted to Leo over the squealing gears.

But Leo was too busy concentrating on trying to drive to respond. Then I heard a dull thud behind me. I turned to look through the perspex window and all but went into a hysterical decline when I saw O'Rourke glaring in at me.

'He's in the back!' I screamed. 'He's in the van with us.'

He had jumped in through the open back doors. Now he was hammering at the chipboard to break through.

'Hang on,' Leo shouted again.

This time the van shot forward and didn't lurch to a halt. Over the rough track we bounced, O'Rourke still hammering at the chipboard. I searched the dark outside for any sign of Jamie, but there was only the thick blanket of black night. I mouthed a prayer that he'd given Mossy the slip. He'd done that, run off I mean, to give Leo and me a chance. I realised it was all the more important that we should get help back here as soon as possible. In desperation I lowered the window and shouted to the dark void, 'We'll be back with help, Jamie. Keep going. We'll be back with the gardai.' Maybe that would scare off Mossy.

Leo was lop-sided as he pressed his foot to the accelerator. Trees and ditches flashed by in a blur. And all the while O'Rourke hammered at the chipboard. I pressed my back to it as if to give it extra strength, but I knew that it wouldn't hold out much longer.

With a bone-crunching thump, the van veered from the track and on to the road.

'Do you know where to go?' I shouted.

Leo didn't take his eyes off the road, his arms were spreadeagled across the steering-wheel. 'Yes,' he shouted back.

This was the small boy I had sworn to protect, the small boy who could add 'save ourselves' to his list of causes, driving like a miniature Nigel Mansell.

As we turned a bend, I let out a cry of relief as the lights of the town loomed ahead. My joy was short-lived. The sound of splintering wood behind me announced that O'Rourke's desperate tearing at the chipboard had paid off. The whole thing was loosening and we could hear O'Rourke's grunts as he tore at it. I looked ahead. The town suddenly didn't seem so near. Calm, keep calm, I tried to tell myself.

O'Rourke had now broken through with a roar of

triumph and his hands were grabbing the wheel from Leo. Leo was so precariously perched that it would only be seconds before he lost control. Sod calm – stir up anger, I thought. I looked about for something, anything to fight off O'Rourke. On the dashboard was one of those things that you light cigarettes with. We had one in our car and I'd often used it to burn holey patterns on paper. I snatched it and pushed it into O'Rourke's face. The shock made him recoil.

'Keep going,' I roared at Leo. All that anger I'd been saving came nicely to the surface and I twisted in my seat to do my gloriously, savagely alley-cat battle with The Enemy. I shoved the cigarette-lighter up his nose. His hand came forward to fend me off and I caught it, sinking my teeth into his foul-tasting flesh. The van was career-

ing all over the road and several cars swerved to avoid us. O'Rourke tore his hand from my mouth.

'I have AIDS!' I screamed. 'You're going to DIE!'

Out of the side of my eye I could see that the landscape had changed. We were in town!

'Leo!' I shouted. 'We're here. Stop. Before we crash.'

Leo ignored me and kept driving. I couldn't hold off O'Rourke any more. He'd thrown the chipboard aside and was now reaching to wrench Leo from the wheel.

'Maeve!' Leo shrieked. 'Hold tight!' And, with his two legs stretched to get his feet to the brakes and the clutch, he twisted his whole body to manoeuvre the steering-wheel. With a screech, the van slammed into a wooden fence. I just vaguely heard splintering noises before I was thrown backwards against the dash. O'Rourke was tossed between Leo and me and his head thumped off the windscreen. Leo, because he was so small, simply slithered under the steering-wheel. The sudden silence was uncanny.

'Are you all right?' My voice came out in a sob as I called to Leo. 'Leo, are you all right?' I felt every drop of life drain from my body when he didn't reply. 'Oh, God. Leo!'

O'Rourke was stirring now. He withdrew his head, bloody in the street light, and began to make a move to get out. He pushed me to one side roughly and stumbled unsteadily to the door. All I could think of was Leo.

'Leo!' I shouted again. There was a movement under the steering-wheel and a filthy face beamed out at me.

Relief! No words, not even mine, could describe the joy at seeing him. 'You little brat!' I cried. 'You maggot! Why didn't you answer?'

'I was checking to see if I was alive ...' he began. But I'd smothered him in a hug by then.

Now there were people gathering around. Gardai, several of them in shirt sleeves, were pulling open the door.

'That was quick,' I said, surprised. Then, when I looked out, dazed, I realised that Leo had driven straight through the wooden fencing outside the garda station. He'd known where he was going all right. Hands were helping us down and lots of people were talking at once. We were both carried into the station where blankets materialised and we were cocooned before we knew what was happening.

When the fog began to clear from my senses, I remembered O'Rourke and Jamie.

Jamie! He was still out there in the bog with a baseball-bat-wielding thug. I threw the blanket aside and tried to stand up.

'Easy there now,' a blonde ban-garda was saying. 'The doctor will be here in a moment ...'

'No!' I shouted. 'You don't understand. Jamie is out there.'

'Where? Is there someone else in the van?' A look of concern crossed her face and she turned to one of her colleagues.

'No! He's in the bog. He's being chased by Mossy. He'll be killed ...'

By now Leo had joined in the hysterical outburst. They tried their best to calm us, but we shouted louder.

'Quiet!' someone shouted eventually. The ban-garda tried to put the blanket around me again, and I shrugged it away. I was hyperventilating, which means that my breath was coming in short bursts.

'Calm down and try to tell us, dear,' she said.

I forced myself to be cool. 'There's a man out there in the bog ...'

'Maher's bog,' Leo interrupted. 'He's chasing after Jamie. He's going to kill him.'

'Nobody's going to get killed, son,' one of the other gardai said. 'Just take it easy and tell us why you were driving that van.'

'For crying out loud!' I exploded. 'There IS going to be murder. You don't understand ...'

'You're getting hysterical again,' the ban-garda said in a soothing voice. In a lower tone she muttered to someone, 'Any sign of that doctor?'

The door swung open and another uniform strode in. He stopped when he saw us. 'Leo!' he exclaimed. 'What's happening here? Your folks are over in Mr McLaren's. They're worried sick. Rang me at home and I was just coming in to organise a search ...'

'Sergeant O'Brien,' Leo looked relieved, 'you've got to get to the bog. There's a thug after Jamie ...'

'We have to go now before it's too late,' I put in. 'Please. Just come. We'll tell you in the car on the way. But you've got to come.' Leo was nodding in agreement.

'I know this lad,' the sergeant said to the others. 'He's my son's pal. He doesn't make up yarns, do you Leo?' He sat down beside him and said patiently, 'Now tell me very simply what's been happening. Are you in some sort of trouble?'

'Yes!' said Leo. 'I mean Jamie is.'

With several stops and starts, we got most of the story across to the disbelieving faces. Jamie. We had to find Jamie.

'He'll be dead and buried in a bog-hole if you don't come now,' I said.

Suddenly there was action.

'Ring McLaren's place,' said the sergeant to the bangarda. Other phone calls were made and everybody sprang into action.

'I'm coming too.' I got up. But, now that the adrenalin had stopped flowing, I realised that there was a throbbing pain – in my rear end. I put my hand to my left hip and nearly passed out when I felt a hot stickiness. Well, all right then, I DID pass out. I'd been to hell and back, fought like a tiger and discovered courage to match any mega-heroine you care to mention, and here I was, passing out at the sight of a few drops of blood. Well, I suppose, it's different when it's your own.

16

At Kildioma Hospital

They had just finished stitching me up after fishing bits of glass out of my bum when Jamie, in a state of exhaustion and covered in black, boggy mud, and Leo were brought into the surgery in the small Kildioma Hospital.

'Oh, lads!' I almost leapt off the table with delight. Nothing else mattered now. The three of us were safe.

There was a commotion outside. The door burst open and Aunt Brid burst in, followed by Jim and a worried looking Mr McLaren. Jim ran straight to Leo and swept him into his arms, burying his face in the smiling dolphin. Leo held on to him with his skinny little arms as if he'd never let him go again. Aunt Brid looked on, several kinds of relief flooding her face. Very touching, but didn't anyone care that I was lying face down on an operating table, scarred for life? As if she read my thoughts, Aunt Brid rushed over to me.

'Maeve! we were ... oh, Maeve.' She broke down and blubbered. The embarrassment of it. Tears rolled down my cheeks as well. Just the physical pain in the butt, you understand; I'm not given to heavy scenes. However we were saved from further displays of emotional melodrama by the doctor ordering everyone out.

'Hey! Not me,' I shouted as a nurse began to wheel me through the double doors. 'I'm part of this. I want to know what happened. Jamie! Leo! Tell them to leave me here.'

Jamie was sitting with his head hanging down, the

picture of exhaustion, barely registering the pat on the shoulder his grandad gave him before leaving. He looked up as I was being wheeled by. I stretched out my hand and he gave me a tired five-finger slap.

Outside the surgery several gardai filled the small waiting-room. There was a buzz of talk.

'Did you get him?' I asked. 'Did you get O'Rourke?'

'Not now, dear,' said the nurse who was wheeling the trolley. 'In the morning.'

'But I have to know.' I twisted around and was stopped short by an excruciatingly sharp pain in my left buttock. 'Did you get to the ferry and stop our heritage being sold …?' Blast, had the woman no pity? Aunt Brid blew me a kiss and indicated that I calm down. What was wrong with these people? Didn't they know that there were killers out there and that Ireland was being stripped of her old stuff?

'Why didn't you at least let me ask them a few measly questions?' I asked her as she helped me into a starchy white bed. She was a plump woman, what my father would call 'homely', and her arms were soft. 'This is serious stuff. You don't understand …'

She smiled and pulled out a trolley from a corner of the small ward.

'And what are you doing with that thing?' I growled as she shot a spurt of liquid into the air from a syringe. Now this I needed like a hole in the head. 'Hold on, now,' I protested. 'I don't actually …'

But she ignored me and shot the ruddy thing into my arm. Then she patted my pillow.

'That will relax you and give you a good night's sleep,' she said.

'I don't want to relax,' I retorted. 'Thanks anyway.' (A lady never forgets her manners). 'But I want to know ...'

She just smiled at me and went out. Cow! How was I supposed to sleep without knowing how Jamie was? Whether they'd caught Mossy and O'Rourke? And the antique stuff, had they managed to save the antique stuff – our national heritage, our chunk of history? The images in my mind became very confused and I felt a warm, pleasant flow of tiredness embrace me. Images of Leo and Jamie, Jamie and Leo, two spunky fellows whose standards of courage came almost up my own. Jamie, the grim determination on his face as he shouted 'Now!' and set the wheels of escape in motion. Jamie ... Jamie ... brave, exhausted Jamie, covered in bog mud ...

The door opened quietly and the nurse's face loomed in my half sleep. 'The gardai have just brought in that O'Rourke man,' she whispered. 'His head is being stitched up at the moment. Thought you'd like to know.'

I tried to nod, but my head wouldn't work. 'Ta,' I slurred. I hoped they'd use a blunt and rusty needle.

The beautiful Miss Morris felt frantically about and grasped at a gnarled tree root. How long could she hold on before her strength gave out and she was sucked into the quagmire?

'Alas!' she cried out to the night. 'Tonight I'll probably meet with the drowned Spanish sailors as we walk to eternity down the long tunnel to where all our ancestors await us in their white frocks. All is lost.' But, hark! What was that? A voice. Were there more villains passing this way? A distant lantern waved to and fro. Someone was calling. She strained her ears.

'Miss Morris, Miss Morris,' she heard. Her heart jumped.

She knew that voice! There was no mistaking the rich, plummy tones of Lord Chiselchin..

'I'm here!' she cried. 'Over here.'

But the wind had caught her voice and there was no response. The voice kept calling her name. Her hand was losing its grip on the tree root. Her strength could no longer hold out. She was slipping ... slipping ...

With one last, desperate surge of energy, she cried out, 'Lord Chiselchin! Lord Chiselchin,' as she felt the cold slime of the boggy mire fill her nostrils. All went black as she surrendered to a murky death. But wait! What was this? Strong hands were pulling her up. She gasped and spluttered politely as her head was dragged free. She wiped the mud from her eyes and blinked at the face of her rescuer. Lord Chiselchin! So, he had heard her after all.

'Oh, Miss Morris,' he exclaimed as he put his arms around her. "Thank goodness I got here in the nick of time.'

'How did you know?' asked Miss Morris. 'What brought you here? I thought you were about your business in the city.'

'I was,' explained Lord Chiselchin as he helped her to her feet. 'But McHayseed, my faithful servant, got wind of the foul deed and told me about it as he was leaving me to the station. He'd known about the whisperings between my wicked uncle and Miss Pickaxe, but feared I would not believe him. I've organised a party of policemen and honest citizens to put a stop to the wrecking. But we don't know which cove these evil people intend to use for their dastardly act. As you know, the coast is full of little coves and we have neither the time nor the numbers to try all of them.'

'But I know!' exclaimed Miss Morris. 'I saw them from my window. They're headed for Skull Cove.'

'Oh you darling girl,' said Lord Chiselchin. 'Clever Miss

Morris! Now all will be well. But we must hurry back to the village where the search party is mustering.'

He glanced down at Miss Morris's feet and, in the light of the lantern, saw her foot wrapped in the torn petticoat.

'I lost my shoe climbing up the cliff,' she explained.

'You poor, brave girl!' he said. He picked her up in his strong arms and carried her across the boggy land.

'You still haven't told me how you came to be here, on the moor,' said Miss Morris.

'I was concerned for your safety when I heard that my uncle and Pickaxe were in cahoots to do this awful thing and have me blamed. I knew then that Grabgreed would stop at nothing to take over my estate. I feared for you and, of course, young Edward. When I rushed to the Pink Room, I saw that the secret door was open, so I came the same way, praying all the while that I was not too late.'

'Oh, Lord Chiselchin,' swooned Miss Morris.

'Oh, Miss Morris,' sighed Lord Chiselchin.

By the light of the lantern, she marvelled at his handsome face. He looked more dashing now than ever, even with his clothes covered in mud. She noticed the way that his chin jutted out, giving his lower lip a decisive assertiveness. His nose was slightly squashed in the middle, broken, she presumed, in some past skirmish, causing his looks to fall short of being too angelically handsome. She couldn't stand angelically handsome men.

Soon the lights of the village came into view. The police and citizens had gathered in the square.

'Skull Cove!' shouted Lord Chiselchin. 'Thanks to brave Miss Morris here, we know that the evil act is to be carried out at Skull Cove.'

The people cheered. Lord Chiselchin set the beautiful Miss

Morris down beside a plump, homely lady. 'Good Mrs. Buttercup will see to you,' he said. 'You need care and rest. We shall be back shortly.'

'What about you?' Miss Morris clutched his hands. 'Let me come with you. Your uncle is a dangerous man. Besides, I know the way ...'

Lord Chiselchin smiled and kissed her dainty, grimy hands. 'You forget I grew up in these parts,' he said. 'I surely know the way to Skull Cove. Get some rest, my sweet. I'll return shortly.'

The beautiful Miss Morris watched in anguish as her brave Lord set off, leading the just citizens to apprehend the evil mob.

'You come along with me, dearie.' Homely Mrs Buttercup put her arms around Miss Morris and led her into her cosy home.

Later, her wounds dressed and her beauty once more restored, Miss Morris lay propped up with big, downy pillows on a patchwork-covered bed. She put aside the tray which Mrs Buttercup had brought her. The roast leg of chicken had been delicious and the home-made strawberry mousse out of this world. Then she felt a sweet drowsiness come over her. She tried to stay awake, she must stay awake to be told of the outcome of the events tonight. But exhaustion overcame her and she fell into a deep sleep, to dream of her love, her Lord Chiselchin.

17

Fame and Farewell

We were sitting in the conservatory at Jamie's place – well perhaps sitting is not quite the right word; I wasn't doing much sitting these days. I was perched on the window ledge in such a way as not to let my injured part touch the wood. It was the first day we could really relax after the recent events. There had been the expected publicity with photographers flashing cameras in our faces and people shoving microphones up our noses. The gardai shuffled us about thither and yon, to make statements and identify the creeps, who'd all been rounded up. O'Rourke had quickly been found, wandering down the street in a concussed state after the crash. Mossy was picked up later that night. He'd stolen a car and was trying to get to Rosslare. The ferry had actually got underway when the gardai were alerted, but it was made to turn and come back into port. The truck was found and all the stuff recovered. Fergus and company were nicked.

It was a neat scam, carried out by a network of criminals placed in strategic parts of the country. Masterminded by so-called respectable pillars of the community, like O'Rourke, stuff was being ripped off from ancient sites and monuments and even old churches that were still in use. O'Rourke, being an auctioneer, had laid hands on the manuscript of the history of the abbey many years before. He did his research and found that it was supposed to be the only copy but, as Mr McLaren

133

explained to us, a second copy had been made before the dissolution of the monasteries back in the time of Henry the whatsit – the fat one with the headless wives.

O'Rourke realised that the secret chamber would be ideal for storing the stolen property from the whole region. Nobody could possibly know about it, he thought, and the only people who went to the abbey were the odd tourist or dusty historian. So he and his team used to collect stuff over a year or more and, when they had a reasonable amount, the shipment would go out among the fertiliser sacks to eager buyers, mainly in Germany, Japan and America. All innocent and above board. Then the whole process would start all over again.

(You could understand some wealthy Irish-American wanting a bit of the ould sod to add a touch of class to his hi-tech penthouse, but where the Germans and Japanese came into it beats me. At any rate, a lot of dosh was involved.)

As if that wasn't bad enough, O'Rourke's crew used go to people in large crumbling mansions and, posing as important antique dealers, would rip them off by paying a pittance for valuable old stuff. The scam there was to offer maybe a hundred pounds for some junky rubbish like great-aunt Mathilda's ear-trumpet. Then the so-called antique dealer would say, 'Throw in that old bust of Daniel O'Connell and we'll give you another fifty quid.' (Daniel, of course, being worth twenty times that). Then he would be carted back to the abbey to be included in the next shipment.

The whole thing seemed foolproof, except for one little thing – Leo's house. It was the only house that over-looked the abbey. Leo's family were the only ones who would be able to spot activity at funny hours. The solution was to buy Brid and Jim out (the money would be peanuts to O'Rourke) and install Fergus in the cottage. It was O'Rourke who had recommended Fergus to Mr McLaren to manage his stables. Very neat. I'd scrubbed my teeth several times over in case any of O'Rourke's evil stuck to my molars after biting him. Still, it had been worth it. Maybe he'd get infected after all and his hand would get gangrene or leprosy and drop off. They say the human bite is the most dangerous of all.

Celebrity status was nice – for a while. But we were getting slightly cheesed off with saying the same old stuff over and over. Besides, no matter how much I practised my sexy poses beforehand, the camera always seemed to make me look like an Addam's Family extra.

Leo seemed to have taken on a new life. Apart from the euphoria surrounding the three of us, his private cloud of tension had completely lifted. 'Leo has laid his ghost,' Aunt Brid confided to me when she came to my room the night after our thrills and spills. 'He has finally accepted his father's death and sorted out where Jim fits into his life. Praise the Lord. Now we can get back to being a family again.'

As I said, that's what I like about Aunt Brid, she always talks to me like I'm an adult.

We never found out what O'Rourke had intended to do with us that night. He said he was just going to hold us there, in the bog, until things had blown over. But I think everyone knew better, even if they couldn't prove it.

The beautiful Miss Morris awoke from her slumber as Lord

Chiselchin entered the candlelit room. His face was muddy, but triumphant.

'All is well,' he said, taking her hands in his. 'We got to those evil people before they could carry out their dastardly plot. The whole gang has been rounded up and are in the clink – in the village dungeon. The ship has docked safely and the captain wants to thank you personally, and present you with a bundle of gold ingots. You are a brave heroine, my dear.'

'It was what any decent citizen would have done,' said Miss Morris.

'Now my poor brother's name has been cleared,' continued Lord Chiselchin.

'What do you mean?' asked Miss Morris.

Lord Chiselchin sighed and told her his story – the story of the awful events that took him so frequently to the city and away from his beloved Manor House.

It seemed that Charlie, his younger brother, was in prison for a murderous crime which (unknown to him) Uncle Grabgreed and Pickaxe had pinned on him. Lord Chiselchin, who had studied law – even though he didn't need to since he was a Lord – spent his time in the city and in the prison trying to get together a case to clear his brother. That explained his worried frown and the long sessions in his study.

'Pickaxe has confessed all,' continued his lordship. 'She broke down under strong questioning and told how Grabgreed, my father's stepbrother, had been using the cove for years as a store for stolen and smuggled goods. Then, when he tired of that business, he'd got the great idea of implicating my brother and me so that he could take my house and land. All he has now,' he added with a grim expression,' is a narrow cell where he will spend many years. And deservedly so. Now my brother can get back to the work he loves – he's an explorer, and I can

get back to running my beloved estate. We owe it all to you, Miss Morris.'

'I said, do you want another sandwich?' Jamie was asking.

'What? Oh, no thanks. I'm full.'

Mrs O'Toole had done us proud with what she called a Celebrity Tea. A summer shower had just stopped and the sun was shining through the drops of rain on the conservatory roof. The smell of recently mown grass wafted in through the open door. Fat, red flowers and skinny yellow ones bowed their heads in the flower-bed outside. Another time, another life – like five days ago, I wouldn't have noticed things like that. Or, if I did, I'd knock the scene. Maybe I was going soft. But I think I was just glad to be alive.

Jamie's right hand was bandaged. That night, he'd run through thorny brambles that grew along the bog track. He'd kept the glow of the town lights in his sight all the time he was running. He'd stumbled on the stony track and tripped over tufts of grass, but he kept on going. Mossy had no light, so at least there was that advantage. And Jamie was very fit. 'All those torturous rugby training sessions at school paid off,' he grinned. He'd kept well ahead of the unfit Mossy. When he came to the main road, he'd taken a chance and flagged down a passing car. As luck would have it, it was a woman on her way to town to pick up her kids from a disco.

'Please,' he cried. 'Take me back down the bog track. Two friends. Thugs have them. Hurry!'

Although he had seen the truck taking off, he didn't know that we were in it. He thought we might still be in

the bog at the mercy of Mossy or O'Rourke or, worse still, corpsed in a bog-hole. He hadn't heard me shouting to him. Quick thinking, the woman drove straight to the garda station. Jamie felt confused emotions when he saw the Hiace, wrecked and steaming, stuck in the station fence. Inside he'd been met by his anxious grandad, along with Aunt Brid who had raised the alarm. She rang Mr McLaren when we didn't arrive home for tea. She thought we'd had lunch there and didn't feel concerned until tea-time.

'They'll never believe us,' I said.

'Who?' asked Leo, opening a sandwich and putting it

back because it had ham in it.

'At school. When we go back. They'll never believe our story. It's far out.'

'How come? We've just been plastered all over newspapers and television!' exclaimed Jamie. 'How could they miss it?'

'Oh, they'll have forgotten all that by September,' I replied. 'Their little brains can't hold information for long.'

'They'll believe you, Maeve,' said Leo.

'Me?' I preened, pleased that Leo was at last aware of my powers of convincing conversation. 'You think so?'

'Yeah,' he grinned. 'You've only to show them your scar.'

'You miserable little reptile,' I snorted. 'How would like to go bungy-jumping off a very low bridge with a very long elastic band?'

I was keeping my injury very low key. The glass I had so carefully stored in my back pocket in the loo in O'Rourke's had shattered when I was thrown against the dashboard. At the time I hadn't even noticed. There were eleven stitches holding the jagged wound together. Imagine – carrying the scar from a criminal's lavatory on one's bum for life. I mean, I couldn't even exploit it. Picture the scene at a posh dinner-party in years to come. An awkward lull in conversation and the hostess, Mega-Star Maeve, says, 'Let me tell you about the time I captured a load of criminals.'

Cries of disbelief from the guests.

'I can prove it,' says Mega-Star Maeve. 'I have a scar to prove it.'

'Show us your scar, Mega-Star Maeve,' they'd say.

See what I mean? I sometimes think God has a truly warped sense of humour.

'So,' said Jamie, changing the subject with his usual diplomacy. 'Where will you drive to next, Leo?'

Leo grinned and rubbed the fading bruise on his forehead. 'In the field behind our house,' he said. 'Jim's going to teach me properly.'

'Well you did OK,' said Jamie. 'All the time that Fergus was showing me how to drive, you were calmly taking it all in?'

Leo nodded again.

'Huh,' I said. 'The stupid creep Fergus didn't realise that those driving-lessons would land him in the clink. A lovely twist. Serve him right.'

Mr McLaren appeared at the door and smiled at us. 'Are you right, lad?' he said to Jamie.

The three of us looked at one another awkwardly for a couple of seconds. The bond that had held us so close together over the past few days was about to be broken.

'Do you really have to go, Jamie?' Leo asked.

Jamie nodded. 'Parents,' he said, almost apologetically. He was wearing that Fair Isle jumper that he'd had on the first day we met him. I wished it was only that first day again. 'They're giving me a few days in Paris.'

'Are you sure you wouldn't like to come to the airport with us?' Mr McLaren asked Leo and me.

I shook my head. I didn't like airports, unless I was going somewhere myself. Anyway it would involve sitting for a few hours. But, most of all, I didn't want my last sight of Jamie to be a metal cylinder in the sky. Mr McLaren was putting the cases into the boot of the car. Jamie thumped Leo on the arm. 'Take care, hot-shot.'

'You too,' Leo thumped him back.

I shifted self-consciously as Jamie came over to me. He took my hand firmly in his non-bandaged one. It felt nice. The way he looked at me made me feel really special.

'I'll be back here next year,' he said. 'You can count on that.'

I nodded. Next year was eternity away. 'I'll write to you, zany Maeve.' All the words I wanted to say got totally screwed up somewhere between brain and mouth, so no sound came out. Jamie gave my hand one last squeeze and joined his grandad in the car. As he wound down the window, I suddenly found my voice.

'Enjoy Paris, Jamie,' I called. 'Remember me to the Tate Gallery.' There, let him remember me as a cultured lady who knew about art and stuff.

He grinned and waved. 'I will,' he said.

We stood and watched the car disappear down the avenue.

'That's in London,' Leo said.

'What is?'

'The Tate Gallery. It's in London.'

'It isn't. It's in Paris.'

Leo shook his head. 'It's in London. It was built by a man called Tate who made sugar. I have a book about London.'

'Knowall,' I said. Maybe Jamie hadn't heard me. But I knew he had. Blast! 'You read too many books. You should get out in the air ...'

'And be an airhead, like you,' Leo laughed, running ahead of me towards the hole in the wall.

I made to run after him, but the stitches reminded me

that I was fragile in parts. Well, maybe I didn't know my Tate from my elbow, but I sure had given a bunch of toerags a hard time. I was an all right person.

'Wait,' I called after Leo. 'What freaky muck is your old lady giving us for dinner? Boiled nettles? Dandelion Delight?'

'I love you, Miss Morris,' said Lord Chiselchin. His slightly squashed nose bore a streak of dirt, and the Fair Isle jumper he'd put on against the night chill was ripped. She put out a hand and gently stroked his bruised chin.

'Marry me and be the mistress of Darkling Hall. Be a mother to young Edward who loves you too.'

'Oh, Lord Chiselchin,' sighed Miss Morris. 'I will. I will.'

MARY ARRIGAN lives in Roscrea, County Tipperary. As well as writing books for teenagers, she had written and illustrated books in Irish for younger children.

Her awards include the Sunday Times/CWA Short Story Award 1991; The Hennessy Award 1993; and a Bisto Merit Award 1994.

Dead Monks and Shady Deals is her first book for The Children's Press.

Tony Hickey
Flip 'n' Flop in Kerry
Ireland's most popular pups move in Kerry, where they
meet a sleuthing sheep-dog intent on solving the
mysterious disappearance of Plucky, the wolf-hound,
and his owner. Illustrated by Terry Myler.
96 pages. £2.95 paperback.

Yvonne MacGrory
The Ghost of Susannah Parry
Brian accepts a dare to spend two hours in a haunted
house. But when he comes home, he has changed
utterly. A gripping story involving the paranormal.
Illustrated by Terry Myler.
128 pages. £3.95 paperback.

Terry Myler
Drawing Made Easy
One of Ireland's top illustrators passes on her secrets. A
step-by-step guide covering materials, techniques,
perspective, composition, sketching from life, various
subjects – dogs, cats, horses, trees, flowers, birds, dogs.
48 pages. £3.95 paperback.

Peter Regan
Young Champions
The further fortunes of the five friends. Will Shane
fulfill his promise? Is this Hammer's year to make it?
Can Elaine stand the pace at Juventus? Luke has
problems – is anyone listening? Jake is caught on a
rising tide – will it lead to fame?
160 pages. £3.95 paperback.